RIVER SISTERS,
THE STRANGERS

by
Jan Dearman

For information, or to order additional copies,
please contact:

Beacon Publishing Group
P.O. Box 41573, Charleston, S.C. 29423
800.817.8480/beaconpublishinggroup.com

Publisher's catalog available by request.

ISBN-13: 978-1-949472-47-9

ISBN-10: 1-949472-47-9

Published in 2022. New York, NY 10001.

First Edition. Printed in the USA.

RIVER SISTERS,
THE STRANGERS

This book is dedicated to the youth
who became our parents, grandparents,
great-grandparents …

"… we had everything before us …"

TABLE OF CONTENTS

Chapter 1
September 1941

Nancy assessed herself in the full-length mirror on the back of the closet door. What would others see on this day she considered the first of her adulthood? As a precocious student and early college entrant, she knew what school officials would expect—they carefully had considered her admissions tests, essays, grade reports, and recommendations. But what would they see? Would they see beyond the light brown curls framing an unusually tan face, deep-set emerald green eyes set above prominent cheekbones, and the scar—hardly noticeable Mother said, but to the analytical eyes of an eighteen-year-old girl, a headlight preceding her every movement and word?

She circled her shoulders forward, then back a few times, and stood as tall as she could stretch. *Confidence*, she told herself, a *calm, intelligent reserve.* She raised an eyebrow—*hmm, that's good, Lauren Bacall, no, Katherine Hepburn,* raising the eyebrow again. They must see her as mature, capable, determined, ready to put her whole mind and body into work that had been her dream since the first remembrance of her early childhood, not only preserved in the treasure room of her earliest thoughts, but nurtured and reinforced on occasion by her mother and father.

She truly was thankful, she told herself. Had it not been for talented surgeons at the Children's Hospital in Cincinnati, she would bear the physical and psychological burden of the cleft palate. And Uncle Morgan and Aunt Maddie, the friends who had welcomed the family into their home while in Ohio, had been so encouraging and supportive. They had remained guardian angels and constants in her life since she was a toddler. It seemed she had given them a new receptacle for the love that continued to flow when the vessel of their beloved son, Caleb, was broken, however valiantly, on that foreign ground of conflict and bloodshed that was France in 1918. Fighting under the blue helmet of the French, he was still their "all-American" son. Though his skin was black, his blood ran fresh and red into strange soil. The one blood of God's humanity followed the course of quest for liberty and opportunity on both sides of the Atlantic.

Nancy rechanneled her thoughts to the freedom and excitement she felt on this morning and to the opportunity set before her. She had restrained her impatience for almost a month while college was delayed, schools and public gatherings having been shut down due to an outbreak of polio. Today, though one family in the area was sorrowing over the death of a child, the council's decision to return the city to normalcy prompted other parents to send their children off to school, with prayers that normal, ordinary days would bring joy and dispel fear. Nancy was thankful she was whole, healthy, and ready to begin college and the pre-med and medical programs that would enable her to care for little ones who, like herself, needed some tweaking to face life with confidence and courage.

A rap on the door brought her back to the moment, followed by the voice of her younger brother, Hank: "Hey, Nut Jar, you'd better get going. Don't want to be late for your date with all your dead bodies!"

"Thanks for the reminder, Jug Head—I hear they're all lined up and waiting for me!" Nancy Jewel and John Henry Hodge, or "Nut Jar" and "Jug Head," as they affectionately had labeled each other, were close—more like twins than just brother and sister. She was barely a year old and in Cincinnati for the surgery, when her mother Eliza discovered she, again, was pregnant—already three months. Mother said the weeks in Cincinnati with their friends, Morgan and Madeline, were a beautiful time: they had the friendship and fellowship of the Kendalls, the hope and optimism of a bright future for their daughter, and the surprise of learning another baby was on the way. They had waited such a long time, and now their cup of blessing was overflowing.

Nancy adjusted the straps of her navy jumper, fastened the white buttons on the band encircling her narrow waist, and reached under the skirt to pull the hem of her polka-dotted shirt, so it would be neat, tight, not blousy. She collected her white sweater and bookbag, perused the room to ensure everything was in order, nothing forgotten, and closed the door on her childhood.

Chapter 2

Eliza Hodge was having her third cup of coffee at her desk in the living room, when her husband and children entered to say good-bye before leaving for work and school.

Josh, lunch pail and cap in hand, came directly to Eliza, tilted up her chin, and planted a quick kiss on her lips. "Have a good day, dear. I'll be home in time for supper at six."

"It'll be ready," Eliza responded.

"I'm going to crank up the car and bring it around. You children be ready."

"I love you!" Eliza shouted at the heavy oak front door, closing behind him.

The door opened again, and Josh, grinning, said, "I love you, too—more than you know!"

"Oh, I think I do!" she shouted back with a laugh. Turning her attention to her children, Eliza took Nancy's hand and said, "Nancy, my Jewel, you look lovely today—very neat and professional, and soon they'll realize what a fine mind you've got behind that pretty face."

"Thanks, Mom. I just want them to know I'm going to be a capable physician."

"Oh, they'll know it."

Nancy replied, "That's a long, hard way down the road—but if I've got the determination of the McNeal women, I'll do it." Nancy hugged her mother and turned to follow her father out the door.

"Sure enough," Eliza agreed, hiding the pride about to burst from her. She continued, "And, young Mr. Hodge, are you ready to get this junior year underway? This is an important one—getting close to graduation." Eliza held out her arms to Hank and asked, "You're not too old to give Mom a hug and kiss?"

"Never, Mom—just not in front of the guys." Hank gave his mother a hug and bussed her cheek. "I'll be home a little later after school. Les and I are going to work out in the weight room."

"Okay. But be home in time to clean up before dinner. Have a good day."

The door closed behind her family, and Eliza smiled the smile of one in complete contentment for all she had, all she loved. She knew she had to keep a tight hold on the joy of each day—life was so fragile, so transitory. She felt warm and secure in this time and place, and she wished she could freeze their ages and circumstances. Yet, she knew returning to the river house when Hank graduated—the house where Nancy Jewel was born, would be a sweet, nostalgic homecoming.

Josh had wanted his children to have a proper education, available only to those living in the next county. So, they had bought this house, a comfortable craftsman cottage, not far from their "little blue house" in North Chattanooga, to which they had returned as newlyweds. After the destruction of the flood of 1917, they had sheltered with family until their own river house was constructed. Over the years since Nancy and Hank had been in school in the city, the river house was available to family members and friends on the river, as they married and built their own homes. Louise and her new husband now cared for the place, while planning to move to their own house by the time of Hank's graduation. Eliza smiled at the thought of her sweet, red-haired niece, Louise, and the obvious care she and Tom gave the place. Eliza knew, when the time came to return to the river, their house would be spotless, well-maintained, and alive with precious memories.

Eliza turned to continue the memoirs of her life on the Trail—"the last-known person, and only woman, to have carried mail on horseback in the Chattanooga area," the columnist for the *Free Press* had described her. And now they wanted the feature column written by the mail carrier herself. Thankfully, Hailey Lesley would be editing and rewriting, as necessary.

River Sisters, the Strangers

How dramatically her life had changed, along with the lives of her family on the banks of the river and countless others on both sides of the oceans. On the blank sheet before her, Eliza sketched the familiar doodle of a tree with limbs branching out far and wide, so significant in reality and in symbolism—the tree on the hill, under which she and Josh had courted and made their vows; the tree of family that had spread beyond the borders of anything familiar, during the conflict and industry of a war that had turned the world upside down and had catapulted friend and foe into an inhuman mire of misery; the Tree of Life, that promised hope and healing for all who would seek shelter under its branches.

Eliza sighed. So many years had passed. So much had changed. Yet, she still had, for whatever reason, optimism, hope, a sense of so much yet to be done. Perhaps it was the love and pride she had in her family. The Tennessee was now tamed, thanks to TVA, and Josh had given up his work on the river to work with the shipyard at North Chattanooga managing projects involving the tugs and barges. Soon no one would be left who knew, first-hand, the dangers of the Pot, the Pan, the Skillet, the Suck—or who remembered the lives caught up in the depths and eddies of the old ones' Giver.

And her children—what joy they had given! If Nancy fulfilled her dreams, when still in her twenties, she would be giving other children the same promising future that now was hers. And Hank—just so all-around good, it seemed, at anything he tried. He had not formulated a "dream plan" for the coming years, but, surely, whatever he chose to do, it would be done well. Thankfully, girls were not yet a distraction, at least, not that she was aware. She thought, *He's grown a good two or three inches over the summer and has the muscles of a man. Just wait, Mom!* She laughed to herself and, shaking her head free of intrusion, got back to the article and the page containing it—blank, save for a thoughtlessly sketched tree produced by a thoughtful mind.

Chapter 3

Josh Hodge dropped his children at the curb in front of the high school. "Well, I'll see you two at home." Adjusting the rear-view mirror to see his daughter, he directed: "Nancy, the bus should be here in about ten minutes. Just catch the Signal Mountain bus at the corner of Fourth and McCallie when you're finished for the day. I'm not sure where it stops. Just get off over the bridge at Frazier. I'll pick you up a little after five at the drugstore."

"Will do," Nancy replied, adjusting the strap of her book bag on her shoulder and folding her sweater over her arm.

Josh warned: "And, if you have one of those chocolate milkshakes while you wait, better not let it spoil Mom's dinner."

"Yes, sir!" She leaned across the tan mohair seat of the car and squeezed her dad's shoulder: "Love you, Dad."

"Love you, too, babe," Josh replied.

She got out and closed the door. "See you, Jug Head," she spoke over her shoulder, as she moved toward the bus stop. "Stay alert in Mrs. Taylor's advanced geometry and trig class. It's easy if you pay attention. If you don't, you'll get swamped in a hurry."

Jan Dearman

"Will do, sis."

Hank closed the passenger door, and Josh called through the window, "Hank, love you, son. Have a good day."

Hank, leaning on the door, looked at his dad and said, "You, too, Dad. If you've got any time after supper, let's get out the chess board and play a game. I've got some moves to show you from Fine's edition on openings."

"You're on," replied Josh. "See you at home."

Hank smacked the car door and gave a thumbs-up.

Josh put the '39 Tudor in gear and smiled not only at the smooth growl of the engine, but at the advancing maturity of his son. Josh remembered how Hank had been such a surprise and joy—a happy baby, in love with his sister since the time he could focus on a face. And Nancy—well, her love for Hank was a thing to behold. She adored her "puffect wittle bruver" and made it her responsibility to see to his every need and want. Nancy required constant supervision with her real-life baby doll, and Hank required protection from the rough and tumble love of a toddler. Thankfully, they all had survived to this point where, though the parents missed the mirth of little ones, they could all enjoy and appreciate each other as adults. *Well, almost adults, and enjoy most of the time*, Josh corrected his thinking with a smile.

11

Josh pulled the sedan into the lot at the ship-yard, slapped on his cap, and grabbed his lunch pail. He enjoyed his work and the good pay he received for his experience and expertise, especially at an age when many men were slowing down and looking for quiet pasture. He, also, realized the importance of what he did as a project coordinator with the ship-yard. With escalating tensions with Germany and Japan threatening to draw the US into war, he knew his job could become even more critical, with shipments turning to commodities and supplies critical to military maneuvers and war machines. He prayed "The War to End All Wars" would be the end; but he knew, too often, humans were forgetful, selfish beings, thoughtless of the past, uncaring about the future, and driven by only the lusts of the day.

Josh picked up his pace as he tried to shake off the memory of Morgan Kendall's son, Caleb, a Buffalo Soldier, who trained in Ohio, served in France, and was posthumously decorated by that appreciative foreign nation for giving his service—and his life, on their behalf. *If war comes again, what about Hank?* he thought. Morgan, seemingly, had handled that now long-ago grief—and racial intolerance, with such patient strength of faith and peace. *Could I do it?* Again, he quickened pace and shook his head. *I think I would die if anything happened to either one of those kids—I'd just die.*

Chapter 4

"Leigh! Alice! You've only got five more minutes before you have to leave," their mother called upstairs.

"We're ready. Be right down," Leigh responded, as she pulled the sleeves of her cardigan to cover the bruises on her wrists. She gathered her notebook and the zippered pouch containing her pen and pencils, with just enough room left for a small comb, compact, and lipstick. "You got everything you need?" she asked her sister, who was tying the sleeves of her sweater around her waist.

"I guess," Alice replied. "I just wish we could wear trousers, like the boys."

"Well, you know we can't. Even if the school allowed it, you know Mother wouldn't." Sometimes Leigh struggled to be patient with her younger sister, who cared more for comfort than looks. Leigh thought, if not for Alice's petite form and natural beauty, her curly dark hair and bright blue eyes, she would be an unsightly, rumpled mess most of the time. She, also, might be less able to evade Father's stern brand of discipline.

Rose Ann Burkhart met her daughters, as Leigh bounced down the last couple of steps and took the sack her mother offered, followed by Alice, moving as if her feet and the sack she took were made of concrete.

"Here are your lunches—a ham sandwich, an apple, and milk money. Also, there are oatmeal cookies. You might meet someone you'd like to share with."

Leigh smiled and gave her mother a kiss on the cheek. "I hope I meet somebody who can be a really good friend. I don't like the first day, especially at a new school, when you don't know anybody." Their dad had been transferred from the Chicago area to manage one of the foundries that made Chattanooga an important center for industrial metal works. The girls had already been "new kids" the previous year, at a school on the west side of town. Now, with the move to this roomy house in a quiet residential community north of the river, once again, they were making a new start. Here they lived within walking distance of schools, a drugstore with a soda counter, a dress shop, a five-and-dime, a bakery and grocery store—seemingly, a pleasant, convenient place to live.

"I just never like school, period," Alice complained, dropping the lunch sack into a canvas bag of school supplies.

"Remember, you have each other. And, Alice, wipe that pout off your face. Just be nice and friendly. You'll make friends and have a good time."

Rose ordered, "Turn around now. Let's take a look at you."

"Do I pass muster?" Leigh quipped, as the skirt of the blue checked gingham dress twirled and bloomed around her. Leigh knew the dress was her mother's favorite. She said the color accentuated Leigh's long blonde hair and made her gray eyes seem blue.

"I believe you'll do," her mother replied, turning to Alice, the replica of Rose herself at the age of fourteen. "Alice, your sweater goes on you, not tied around you. You know, you could put a little more effort into your appearance." Rose ran her fingers through the dark ringlets framing Alice's face. "That pretty face would be a lot prettier, if you'd just try to smile."

Alice returned a fake smile, revealing deep dimples that made her look like Shirley Temple, Dad said.

"Remember, just go right out of the drive, to the corner, then, down the hill. Be careful to cross the street at the crosswalk," reminded Rose.

"Mother, I'm almost seventeen, and the school is maybe three blocks away. I think we can manage."

Rose swatted Leigh's backside. "Well, Miss Smarty Pants, go or you'll be late. I'll expect you home within the hour after school lets out. Take care of your sister."

"Mom, I'm a freshman!" Alice protested.

"So, you be sure and act your age." Rose grabbed the arm of her reluctant younger daughter and pulled her close to kiss her cheek. "You behave yourself. You get in trouble at school, you know you'll have bigger trouble when you get home." She watched the girls walk down the drive to the street, calling after them, "Love you girls."

"Love you, too!" called Leigh.

"Love you," agreed Alice.

Students were milling around the gym doors, waiting for them to open with the first bell. Leigh and Alice sat on the low brick wall separating the yard from the walkway.

"Hi, are you girls new this year?" The question came from a girl with strawberry blonde curls swept back from her round face by a green and yellow scarf.

"Yes," answered Leigh. "I'm Leigh Burkhart, and this is my sister, Alice. I'm a junior. She's a freshman."

"Super! I'm Cassie Hawthorne. I'm a junior, too. My cousin's a freshman." She turned to call to a tall, thin girl with long brown hair and glasses, "Hey, Millie, come here." Millie walked over to be introduced. "This is my cousin, Millie Hawthorne.

Millie, this is Leigh Burkhart and her sister, Alice. Alice will be in your class."

"Hi, nice to meet you," Millie replied softly. "I'll show you around, Alice, if you want me to."

"Sure, thanks," Alice agreed.

"Come and meet some of the other girls. They're nice. I think you'll like them, unless you're looking for the popular crowd," Millie added, laughing.

"No, that would be my sister," Alice giggled, punching Leigh on the shoulder.

Leigh stuck her tongue out at her sister, as she stood to go with Millie, and Cassie took Alice's place on the wall.

"Did you just move here?" Cassie asked.

"We just moved to this part of town, from West Side, but we've been in the city for more than a year. We moved here from up North—outside Chicago.

"Wow, big city girl," Cassie laughed. "Well, I hope you like it here. I can show you around and help you get to know some people. We get together down at the drugstore soda bar after school most days, if you can go."

"Sounds like fun. I'll run it by my mom. She likes to have me home right after school."

"Guess it was hard leaving your friends to move over here?" queried Cassie.

"Well, I do miss some of my friends," Leigh admitted, "but I'm glad to meet you."

Cassie nudged Leigh's side and asked, "Did you leave anybody *special*?"

Understanding Cassie's emphasis on "special," she replied, "No, there was no one special. I had some friends who were boys, but no boyfriend."

"See those boys over there?" Cassie pointed to a group of boys playing around the big oak tree in the corner of the yard. "The big blonde guy is my boyfriend, Les Thompson. He plays football."

"Is he a junior, too?" asked Leigh.

"No, he's a senior. He'll be eighteen next month." Cassie sounded proud, as she declared her relationship with the older boy.

Leigh noticed with Les a darker boy in overalls and white shirt with rolled-up sleeves, now suspended and doing chin-ups from a low branch of the tree. He was slightly shorter but appeared almost as muscular as his friend. "Who's the boy hanging from the tree?" she asked with a laugh, as Les poked the boy's ribs, causing him to release his grasp and fall to the ground.

"Oh, that's Hank Hodge. He's in our class. I think his real name is John Henry Hodge, but everybody calls him Hank. He's been Les' best friend since elementary school. Good looking, huh?"

Leigh remarked, "I bet the girls are really after him."

"Well, they'd like to be. He's funny—always teasing the teachers and making jokes, but he's kind of shy around girls. He's also smart—probably makes the best grades in the class. His older sister finished school early and is already starting college. She wants to be a doctor."

"Being smart must run in their family," Leigh responded, then giggled: "He reminds me of Li'l Abner in the comics."

"Not nearly as tall, but just as good looking." Cassie continued, whispering, "Maybe you could be his Daisy Mae. You know, this year our class hosts a Sadie Hawkins Day party in the gym, and the girls can ask the guys to go with them."

Leigh responded with raised eyebrows, a nod and pursed lips, "Maybe."

The bell resounded through the campus as the gym doors opened. Leigh and Cassie made their way inside to the juniors' section, where they would wait for their homeroom assignments. Leigh considered the information from her new friend. She hoped she would be with Cassie in homeroom, but she also thought it would be nice to be near Hank Hodge. Maybe she could break through his shyness. She would sure like to give that a shot.

Chapter 5

Rose Burkhart knew she would relish the next several hours. The girls were in school, and Charles had left in the early morning for a day's work that likely would last until ten tonight—or so he said. Surely, she had an inordinate amount of work remaining—unpacked boxes still stacked in the basement, and she wanted to fix the girls something special for a "first day at school" supper, maybe put a roast in the Dutch oven, make a chocolate cake. But, for now, she could sit on the screened-in back porch for a few quiet moments, alone, with a cup of tea and some oatmeal cookies. She closed her eyes and felt the spirit of freedom promised by the late summer breeze. Hope flickered within her, as she opened her eyes to shafts of sunlight piercing the canopy of trees towering over the backyard. Looking beyond them to the white puffs of clouds floating in the clear blue September sky, she imagined a cleansing of life and memory that would bring peace to her family, to her soul. She wondered how it could be—and when? And what would be the price to stanch the rivulet of evil flowing just below the surface of their "typical" American family?

She remembered a verse of Scripture she had heard as a young girl, when she accompanied her grandmother on Sundays: "Ye shall know the truth, and the truth shall make you free." She knew the truth. Charles Burkhart knew the truth. But the truth they knew had only imprisoned them in a box of misery and distrust, tied up with a pretty red ribbon. It was a package of her choosing, her wrapping, but Leigh was the one who suffered with her. Surely the girls realized the difference Charles made between them—with one, preference at times, yet an unloving severity; with the other, indifference usually, yet sometimes loving playfulness. Rose's desire for some guarantee of safety and provision at a time when she was alone and fearful had brought her to this point, to a perverse security and stability—having a home and the necessities for her children, with the expectation that each day might bring anger, even abuse, to herself or Leigh and, within herself, a passive acceptance of infidelity, as abhorrent as the sin.

From the pocket of her blue-checked gingham apron, Rose withdrew the small worn photos, edges now crumpled and separating into layers. The first was a photo of Rose, very pregnant, with her father, his arm wrapped around the girth that once had been her waist. Rose smiled at the memory: a foot taller than Rose, he looked so proud, probably like any expectant grandfather.

Rose shuffled the photo behind the next one and focused her attention on the young man, so handsome and smiling in his dark blue uniform, brass buttons lining the front of his coat. He held his hat in his hand as he leaned against the fence near the road where his police detective's car was parked. She remembered how he had tried to tame the sandy hair that rustled in the breeze. He said he wanted these pictures to be the first in their baby's album. She turned the photo over to see the words: "My beloved husband, Jack, September 30, 1922—almost nineteen years ago now. He had not lived to see the album or to see Leigh. Two weeks later, two C&O workers found his body near the tracks at Dearborn and Polk. He had one neat bullet hole in the back of his skull.

Rose wiped away the gentle tears streaking her cheeks and put the photos back in her apron pocket. She would return them to their place beneath the tufted blue silk lining of her grandmother's glove box, in the bottom of her hat box on the closet shelf. If Charles found them, he would destroy them, along with the last precious remnants of the life and love she had known.

She had been so optimistic about her relationship with Jack's friend, Charles, who seemed to her an angel of mercy at just the time she needed one. He was soft-spoken and reserved, not at all like Jack, who was talkative, full of energy, and with a grin that would light up any dark moment. Charles came into her life only six months after Jack was killed, as Rose was struggling to provide for herself and for Leigh. Charles was quiet, but kind and solicitous, seemingly completely at ease with a widow with a baby. She was so thankful for his concern and his desire to step into Jack's role as guide and guardian.

Rose remembered thinking, *Surely, friendship and trust can be the foundation of a solid marriage.* She had known excitement, passion, and the willingness to walk through fire for her young love with Jack. What had she learned in the years she had shared with Charles? Friendship must be true, trust must be proven, and marriage without them was a charade of stability, a mask of normalcy, and a measure of misery that tinged her every private moment.

Chapter 6

Nancy settled into a desk on the first tier of the concrete floor of the lecture hall and dropped the heavy bookbag at her feet. Moving aside the Western Civilization and calculus texts and the English literature anthology, she withdrew from the bag the chemistry book and lab manual and placed them on her lap, put her notebook and pencil case on the desk, and prepared to focus on the face and words of the professor. His back was turned to the cacophony of shuffling students, scooting desks, and murmuring voices behind him. Nancy noted the information he had written on the blackboard: *Professor Albright, General Chemistry I, M-W-F, 2:00 P. M.* and, beneath that line of print, *Jeffrey Langston, Lab Instructor, T-TH, 2:00 P. M.* Nancy realized she would be coming to campus just for labs on Tuesdays and Thursdays, but she would welcome the blocks of time in the morning and after lunch to study and complete assignments in the library. The reserved, stately, grande dame of campus buildings was a bastion of learning, where she planned to ensconce herself in studious solitude among the comforting smell of old books and oiled hardwood floors.

A bell rang and the teacher turned to approach the lectern, where he faced the assemblage of students. A wave of silence spread over the room as students noticed his slow, pensive scanning of the rows and faces before him. Nancy wondered if his years of experience had given him some ability to assess the academic worthiness of the quarter's students before the first lesson had even begun. She was glad she had arrived in time to procure a front row seat.

A white-haired, shriveled little bird of a man, with glasses perched on almost the tip of a prominent beak, Professor Albright cleared his throat and crackled: "Good afternoon, ladies and gentlemen." Nancy looked down at the notes page to hide her smile, as she wondered if the instructor was a smoker or if many years of teaching had left his voice akin to the sound of heavy feet on dried leaves. "I am Professor Jedediah Albright, your instructor for this quarter. As you are aware, we will meet at the times indicated on the board. Class will begin promptly at two, and I expect each of you to be in your seat when the bell rings, with your mind in gear to attend to our lecture and discussion." Gripping the sides of the podium, he leaned forward and peered over his glasses, continuing: "If for some unavoidable reason you are late, please enter the lecture hall quietly and unobtrusively and take a seat in the back row. You will be held responsible for all class material you may miss due to tardiness or absence."

The instructor crooked a gnarled finger at a tall, swarthy, bespectacled man, not much older than Nancy, it seemed, who stood and came down the side tier of steps to approach Professor Albright. As he walked, he swept an unruly shock of dark hair from his brow and straightened the knot of a navy-striped tie encircling the white collar standing above a V-neck navy pullover. Putting his hands in the pockets of his gray trousers, he stood next to the podium, where Professor Albright now rested his elbows and clenched his hands.

"Ladies and gentlemen, this is Jeffrey Langston." Mr. Langston nodded. His smile was shy, brief, and uncomfortable, Nancy thought. "Mr. Langston is my graduate assistant and will be supervising your work in the laboratory. He has done excellent work himself, graduated tops in his class, and is well-prepared to see you through your assigned experiments. I expect you to give him your full attention and cooperation and to observe all the safety precautions and procedures he outlines in tomorrow's introduction to the laboratory." Turning to Mr. Langston, Professor Albright said, "Thank you, Jeffrey. You may be excused."

"All right, class, let us begin by turning to the first chapter of the chemistry book that, I trust, you already have in your possession. If you have not obtained one, please, make sure you have it before you leave campus. The bookstore has several remaining in stock. You will be responsible for studying the first chapter and for completing the chapter review and one of the short essay topics that follow. You will be required to submit your written work at the next class meeting Wednesday. Place it in the appropriate tray on the desk." He nodded toward the desk to his left in front of the chalkboard, where four deep trays were aligned, each with a label—*Gen. Chem. I, Gen. Chem. II, Org. Chem I., Org. Chem II.*

Uneasy thoughts began to intrude upon Nancy's focus, as she considered the mounting stack of texts and assignments she had collected on only the first day. She knew she could do the work, but she would have to have time to concentrate—uninterrupted time without distraction. Nancy thought, *This is my life, my work, for years to come—for nearly half as many years as I've been alive!* Then she almost chuckled at the thought of her mother: *I'm Eliza McNeal's daughter—I can do it!*

Chapter 7

Hank and Les filed into the gymnasium with the other students. Seeing Cassie ahead, Les shouted, "Hey, Cass, wait up!" Hank lagged behind as Les maneuvered through the stream of students to join Cassie, who had moved to the side of the hallway and waited with Leigh. Hank had drawn close enough to hear Les' greeting, "Good morning, Cassie Lassie," and to see him buss her on the cheek.

"Les, stop! You'll get us in trouble!" she protested, giggling and touching her face. She surveyed the area to see if anyone reacted to the prohibited "public display of affection." Hank wondered if his face registered the distaste he had for their behavior.

Les laughed and noticed Leigh. "Hi, I'm Les Thompson."

"This is Leigh Burkhart," introduced Cassie. "She's a junior too."

"Pleased to meet you," Leigh said, as she offered her hand to shake his.

"Back at you," he replied with a laugh. Les saw Hank passing by them and grabbed his friend's sleeve. "Hey, Junior Buddy, come here." Hank's expression was both questioning and irritated, as he struggled to catch the notebook nearly snatched from

28

under his arm. He checked above his ear to make sure the freshly sharpened pencil still rested there.

"Hey, Cassie," Hank directed his customary dry greeting to his friend's girl.

"Hank, this is Leigh Burkhart," offered Les. "She's new in your class this year."

Leigh put out her hand again to shake Hank's. "I'm looking forward to getting to know you and to being part of the class."

Hank noticed the hand in his was small and smooth with rose-colored nails. His gaze lingered only briefly on blue-gray eyes sparkling below thick dark lashes. He felt himself flush with embarrassment, as he sought a witty retort. "Well, there's not much to know about me, but we've got a good class." He nudged Les with his elbow and laughed: "We'll be great seniors after this dogface's worthless lot!"

"Enough poor-mouthing about yourself, Hodge. Don't let him fool you, Leigh. He's tops in the class, president of the student council, and captain of the wrestling squad. Beyond that, he's pretty much just a hick river rat," Les laughed, flicking the pencil from behind Hank's ear.

"Les, you muscle-head!" protested Hank, as Cassie and Leigh laughed at the interaction between the two bickering, yet devoted friends. Hank retrieved his pencil and declared as he moved toward the gym door, "Come on, Les, we're going to be late. See you around, girls."

The students moved to their places on the gym bleachers at the direction of Mr. McConnell, the principal, as his voice issued instructions from a microphone that squealed and startled the assembly to a brief silence: "Seniors, you may take seats in the balcony. Freshmen, juniors, and sophomores note the placards on the top railing that indicate your sections. Please move along and be seated as quickly as possible. I am going to call the rolls of the assigned homerooms. When you hear your name, you may be dismissed to go to your homeroom and meet there with your teacher, who will give you further instructions." Mr. McConnell watched and waited for the classes to settle in their places.

"Well, what did you think about Les and Hank?" Cassie whispered to Leigh.

"They really give each other a hard time, don't they?" Leigh laughed, as she arranged the notebook, pouch, and lunch bag on her lap. "They seem nice—and they are hunks!" she grinned at Cassie and winked.

"Oh, they roughhouse and prank each other, but they're probably closer than a lot of brothers. I'd say one would die fighting to defend the other."

With another squeal, the microphone broadcast the voice of Mr. McConnell: "All right, students, let's get quiet, and we'll start with the seniors. The first group to be called will follow Mrs. Taylor to her room: Roberta Adams, William Barnes …"

The girls sat quietly and assessed the seniors as they were dismissed.

"That's Hope Reynolds." Cassie sniffed as she nodded toward a thin brunette wearing a letter sweater. "She's a cheerleader. She's always flirting with Les, but he tells me he ignores her. She obviously doesn't like me, so I know he's honest about that, or she'd be gloating. Oh, look, Les is going to be in Coach Leonard's homeroom. He'll like that. Coach Leonard is a real buddy with Les and Hank— works out with them in the weight room after school some days."

Leigh considered the girls as they filed from the gym. None of them gave her the sharp pang of self-consciousness and intimidation she had sensed in times past. At least for the present, she could feel confident of being above par compared to any of them. Only little above average as a student, she knew her looks were her primary asset.

"See any boys who interest you?" Cassie laughed, interrupting Leigh's assessment of the competition.

As far as the boys were concerned, she hadn't seen any that approached the attractiveness of Les and Hank. "No," she laughed, "looks like Les and Hank are the minority."

"My thoughts exactly," Cassie agreed, giggling.

After a few moments of waiting for the three groups of seniors to be called, Leigh continued their whispered conversation with a sigh, "I hope we are assigned to the same homeroom."

"You mean 'We,' you and me, or 'we,' you and Hank?" Cassie teased.

"How about 'we,' all three of us?" Leigh responded with a grin.

"Now, juniors, please listen for your names to be called," announced the principal.

"Well, here we go," Cassie declared. "Fingers crossed."

Mr. McConnell continued: "These students will go with Mr. Sanders: Renee Adams, Loretta Barnhill, Leigh Burkhart…"

Leigh collected the things on her lap, rising when her name was called. She showed crossed fingers to Cassie and moved to join Mr. Sanders' homeroom.

"…Mabel Ferguson, Alex Gentry, Cassie Hawthorne…"

"Swell!" Leigh muttered under her voice. She tried to slow her pace to hear the names to follow.

"...Regis Herbert, Robert Hereford, Hank Hodge..."

Leigh waited for Cassie to clear the gym doors and grinned as she heard her declare: "Hot diggity! The gang's all here!"

Cassie and Leigh took desks beside each other three rows from the front. When Hank appeared at the door, he glanced at the girls and took a seat behind Alex Gentry, who was near the entrance where Mr. Sanders stood. Closing the door behind Betty Malone, the teacher proceeded to the front of the room, as he directed the class: "Please, be seated and give me your attention." The students settled and became attentive at the authoritative resonance of his deep voice: "I am Mr. Philip Sanders, your homeroom teacher. You will begin your days with me in this room. I trust that won't get you off to a bad start," he smiled. "Every morning, we will begin, of course, with the Pledge of Allegiance and an inspirational thought for the day that I hope will circulate through your minds from time to time as you go about your activities."

Cassie caught Leigh's attention, rolled her eyes, and wrinkled her nose. Leigh responded with a sly smile and turned to check on Hank's reaction. She happened to catch his unsmiling eyes looking at her before he returned his attention to Mr. Sanders' words. The brief interaction left her feeling somehow chastised.

Mr. Sanders said: "Please stand and address the flag." The students stood and, hands over hearts, recited with Mr. Sanders: "I pledge allegiance to the flag of the United States ..."

As she spoke by rote, Leigh glanced again at Hank and noticed his apparent concentration on the flag and the words. His seriousness struck her as a bit odd, even out of place among this group of teenagers. Hearing the final words, "....indivisible, with liberty and justice for all," Leigh sat down and waited for Mr. Sanders to continue with his "inspirational" message. She wondered what words he might find that had the power to inspire her and everyone else in the class, day after day, for an entire school year.

With an air of solemnity and dignity, Mr. Sanders took a thick, leather-bound book from his desk and announced: "Let me read this far too lengthy, but famous first sentence of a novel that some of you may study this year in English literature." Mr. Sanders' voice was beautiful in its deep, rich tones, as he began: "It was the best of times, it was the worst of times, it was the age of wisdom, it was the age of foolishness, it was the epoch of belief, it was the epoch of incredulity, it was the season of

Light, it was the season of Darkness, it was the spring of hope, it was the winter of despair, we had everything before us, we had nothing before us, we were going direct to Heaven, we were all going direct the other way...'" Mr. Sanders suddenly slapped the book closed and declared: "That one sentence goes on for another thirty-four words. Though Mr. Dickens describes the period of the French Revolution, it seems to me his words are an apt description of the period of teenage known as the 'Junior Year.' He placed the book back on the desk and looked up with a grin at the quizzical faces of his class.

Mr. Sanders chuckled: "Believe it or not, I was once a teenager. I know the ups, 'the best of times,' and the downs, 'the worst of times,' that come with being in that amorphous stage between childhood and adulthood. This junior year will be busy, full of preparation for graduation and, perhaps, for making choices that will affect the rest of your adult life. I'm not just here to call roll and make announcements, but to be a good listener, a helper, even a confidante, should you need one. Ours will be a relationship of mutual respect. I always will enforce the rules, but I will be a fair and impartial sounding board, if needed. Can we work together on that basis?"

Mr. Sanders waited until he was satisfied with the "Yes, sirs" and nodding of heads. Taking the roll book, he directed: "When I call your name, raise your hand, and I will give you your class schedule." He added wryly: "A word of warning: I'll see several of you again later in the day for World History."

Leigh wondered if this man could be as warm and trustworthy as he seemed. He didn't seem to be much like her father—really, the only adult male that had any influence in her life, since her mother's father had passed. Stern, humorless, unsmiling except when taunting or sarcastic, her father was rarely loving and warm, except with Alice on occasion. And even Alice, aware of the woeful lack of lovingkindness shown her mother and older sister, didn't reciprocate fully the affection of those few fatherly moments.

Leigh's thoughts were interrupted by "Leigh Burkhart." Leigh raised her hand and took from Mr. Sanders the sheet listing her classes for the day.

"Miss Burkhart, I believe you are a new arrival this year. Welcome. We hope you will have a pleasant and productive couple of years here at North Side."

"Thank you, sir," Leigh responded. "I believe I will."

Nodding toward Cassie, he added, "It looks like you have the makings of a good friend in Miss Hawthorne. She and I are old friends from last year's American History class." Cassie blushed and laughed with the class, when he added, "She's a fine girl and a capable student, but she's a talker. Don't let her lead you astray, especially in my World History class."

When Mr. Sanders came to Hank's name, he teased, "And now, Mr. John Henry Hodge, I hope you won't follow in your sister's footsteps and leave us before the time. We need your leadership, especially to take us to State Finals this year and next."

"No, sir, no plans for that. I'm not as adventurous and ambitious as Nut Jar!"

Mr. Sanders grinned and responded, "And maybe Jug Head needs more time to mature."

Hank and the class lost themselves in laughter at Mr. Sanders' quick retort. Leigh thought, *I think I'm going to be happy here. Already, I don't feel like a stranger.* She watched Hank as he regained his composure and noticed his first glance away from Mr. Sanders was directed toward her. This time, for a moment, their eyes shared an unguarded smile.

Chapter 8

Eliza jumped as the screened kitchen door slammed behind Hank, who entered breathless, flushed, and dripping with perspiration. "John Henry Hodge, you're going to stop my heart one of these days!"

"Sorry, Mom," Hank laughed through his gasps, as he opened the ice box for a bottle of cold milk.

"What are you doing here at this hour? I thought you were going to work out in the weight room."

Hank chugged the bottle and set it in the sink. "Whew," he sighed as he sat on the kitchen stool at the end of the counter where Eliza stood peeling potatoes. "Les wanted to meet Cassie at the soda fountain, and Coach Leonard said he had a lot of paperwork to do. So, I decided I'd just get some exercise and run home."

"Where are your books?"

"No, need for books—no assignments on the first day of school," he grinned.

Eliza warned: "Better enjoy the free time. I imagine there'll be plenty of work before the week is out." She dropped the potatoes into the pot of water standing ready on the stove.

Jan Dearman

"What are we having for dinner? I'll be near starvation by the time Dad and Nut Jar get home."

"We should be eating by six or shortly there-after," Eliza replied. "If it won't spoil your dinner, you can have a couple of cookies and some more milk," she added, nodding toward the pottery apple cookie jar on the sideboard. "Oh, and we're having baked pork chops, mashed potatoes, green peas, fruit salad, and homemade rolls your Aunt Lindy made."

"Wow, sounds great!" Hank declared. "Some special occasion?"

"Well, it's your sister's first day of college and the start of your big junior year. I thought we ought to celebrate a bit. And look under the cake cover over there when you get your cookies."

Hank pulled up the wooden knob on the alu-minum cover to reveal a triple layer yellow cake with chocolate buttercream frosting. "Oh, super! My fa-vorite! But who took the first slice?" he questioned, noting the sliver removed to reveal the three layers.

Eliza laughed, "Well, I had to make sure it was worth serving to my family. I might have left out an important ingredient." She looked at Hank and winked, "But I didn't."

Hank sat again on the stool with his cookies and another bottle of milk. The kitchen was quiet as Hank seemed to assess the chocolate chips remaining after each bite of cookie and gulp of milk.

Eliza noted her son's sudden silence and pensiveness. "How are Les and Cassie doing?"

"Oh, you know, they are 'in love,'" Les said with a sneer. "Just like today—working out in the weight room lost out to his meeting Cassie for a soda."

"Well, son, you may just find someone special before long—and you'll understand how Les feels. He'll always be your best friend, but Cassie may one day be his wife. If so, she will be the most important person in his life. You'll always have to take second place, at best."

"Yeah, I know," he muttered before correcting himself, "Yes, ma'am."

"Anything interesting happen at school today?" Eliza continued.

Hank paused to think and then offered: "Well, Mr. Sanders is my homeroom teacher. He was kind of funny today." Hank recounted the teacher's interaction with Cassie and his reference to Nancy's college entrance and to Hank as "Jug Head." Then, Hank added, "We had a new girl in class—a transfer from West Side. She and Cassie seemed to be hitting it off really well."

"Well, that's nice. I'm sure it must be hard to leave friends and start at a new school in the junior year. Did you introduce yourself and welcome her to North Side?"

"Les and I met her this morning. She was with Cassie before school started," he hedged nonchalantly, shrugging his shoulders.

Reading Hank's demeanor, Eliza huffed, turned toward her son, and gesticulated, paring knife in hand: "Now, Hank Hodge. I take that to mean you were not very friendly and welcoming. Was that because you are not a nice person, or because she was a girl?" She noticed Hank's ears turning red with embarrassment. "Well, I know you are a nice person. I also know you'll be seventeen this school year, and it's time for you to learn you are going to have to deal with all people in this world, including females. You be a gentleman and be polite, but don't be afraid."

Hank took in his mother's words and responded, "Yes, ma'am."

Eliza returned to her meal preparation, laying pork chops out in a baking dish. "You just choose your friends wisely, male or female—friends you can trust, who will not corrupt your good morals. You always be a leader. Look out for the welfare of others, but you bring them up to your Christian standards."

Hank came to stand behind Eliza and wrapped his arms around her waist. "Yes, ma'am, Ma Preacher," he teased. "Thought sure I was going to get a knife between the eyes there for a moment."

"Hank Hodge, get your sweaty arms off me and go get cleaned up!" Nancy laughed, flicking a dish towel at his hastily retreating backside.

Chapter 9

"Hey, Leigh! Come join us," Cassie called out, as Leigh and Alice opened the door to the drugstore. Cassie and Millie were sitting at a table near the soda fountain, and Les had moved to pull two chairs from an adjacent table.

"Here you go, girls. Join us. We're just reviewing the first day of my last year at North Side High." Les waited for Leigh and Alice to be seated and then said to Alice, "You must be Leigh's sister. I'm Les Thompson. I go with Cassie Lassie, here—kind of like salt and pepper."

"Surely, you can do better than that! Why not kind of like Scarlett and Rhett?" Cassie suggested in her finest Southern drawl.

"Oh, my dear," Les mocked dramatically, "I'll think about that tomorrow. Tomorrow is another day."

"Oh, Les, you can be such a fat-head!" Cassie laughed.

Turning to Leigh and Alice, Les asked, "Well, do you girls think you're going to like it here?"

Leigh replied, "The first day has been swell. I've felt right at home, thanks mainly to 'Scarlett' here," she grinned as she nudged Cassie.

"Well, we aim to please," Les said. "How about you, Alice?"

"It's been a good day. Millie has been nice enough to stick by me much of the day, to help me get my bearings." Alice smiled at her new friend, who smiled in return and asked, "Want to get some ice cream?" The two younger girls moved to the soda bar, as Alice teased, "We'll leave you upper classmen, so we can go engage in more mature conversation."

Les grabbed his heart and exclaimed, "Oh, you got me! That hurt!"

Their laughter faded, and Cassie asked Les, "Guess this is the last time you can meet here for a while because of practice?"

"Yes, Cass, afraid so. The coach gave us today off. He's got a lot of first day paperwork and planning to do. But, beginning again tomorrow, it's 'start early, stay late' most every day."

"What are your plans after graduation, Les?" Leigh inquired.

"This summer I plan to work with my dad in the hardware store. I'd like to think some scouts would check out my games this year and offer a scholarship, at least to a small college in the area." Shaking his head, he declared, "College takes a lot of dough!" Putting his arm around Cassie's shoulders, he added, "Of course, if I see I can make a good living at a steady job, I may just sweep Scarlett here off her feet, marry her, and start producing and coaching my own football team!"

"And what if you only produce girls?" Cassie teased.

"We'll they'll be pretty, like you, but tough like me, and we'll put them in pink uniforms! They'll be unbeatable!" Les retorted.

The younger girls rejoined them, interrupting their laughter, and Alice advised: "Leigh, we'd better get going. Mom wanted us back within the hour after school."

"Yes, she'll be concerned if we're too late," Leigh agreed with a sigh.

"Can I walk you girls home?" Les offered.

"No, thanks, Les. We just live across the street and up the hill a few blocks," Leigh replied, as she stood and picked up her bag."

"Oh, hey, Leigh, before you go," he added, "What did you think of my junior buddy, Hank?"

"Well, I didn't really talk to him much. He's in my homeroom and in a couple of other classes— and study hall, I think. He seems nice. Maybe a P.C. with the teachers?"

"Oh, yeah, he's their golden boy. He's more comfortable around teachers than he is around girls. Got to fix him!" Les declared, shaking his head. Then he added with a grin: "Maybe you'd be interested in helping me with that?"

Leigh laughed. "Well, we'll see. Maybe he doesn't need fixing—maybe he just needs some time." Leigh followed Alice out the door, calling after them, "See you guys tomorrow!"

They had crossed the street and were going up the hill when Alice asked, "Who's this 'junior buddy'?"

Leigh answered, "Hank Hodge. Cassie says he and Les have been best friends since elementary school."

"Why does he need fixing?"

"He doesn't. He's just kind of shy around girls."

Alice's curiosity was satisfied only momentarily. "Well, what's he look like?"

"Well, he's not quite as tall as Les, muscular, tanned, dark brown hair, and blue eyes, I think. You'll probably see him on hall monitor duty sometime. He's the president of the student council, and I think they're the ones who check hall passes."

"Is he on the football team?"

"No, he's captain of the wrestling team." Leigh paused, then teased: "You know, if you're interested, you're only a freshman—too young for a junior boy."

Alice laughed. "Oh, I know. I was just check-ing him out in case you want to help Les fix him."

Leigh playfully swung her bag and popped the back of Alice's head. "You silly goose! I don't need a guy who needs fixing!"

Alice hurried ahead a few paces, before turn-ing toward Leigh and walking backward, while con-tinuing her interrogation: "Well, what kind of guy do you want?"

"Who says I want a guy? Do you think I'm khaki-wacky? And you're going to break your neck if you don't turn around!"

Alice continued to taunt: "Oh, you wouldn't be wearing that nail polish … and lipstick … and pulling out that mirror all the time to check your hair. You're pretty wacky."

Leigh feigned a chase after her sister, who turned, giggling and running the remaining block into the driveway of the Burkhart home. Leigh laughed at the teasing of her younger sister. She won-dered if Alice would be as childish and playful in a couple of years, when she, too, stood on the brink of adulthood.

Leigh closed the front door behind her and set her bag on the hall table, before entering the kitchen where Rose was pouring batter into a cake pan. Her mother looked up when the bowl had emptied and asked, "Hey, precious, how'd your day go?"

Leigh swiped a finger along the edge of the bowl her mother held out to her. Licking her finger, she said, "Um, chocolate!" Leigh leaned against the sink and replied, "Really well. I met a great girl in my class—Cassie Hawthorne. She's really friendly and a good student. She's going steady with Les Thompson. He's a star on the football team. Cassie's cute—curly strawberry blonde hair and big blue eyes, but she's not at all snooty. We're in the same homeroom. Mr. Sanders is the history teacher. He was nice—he welcomed me to the school. He's also funny. The president of the student council is in my homeroom. He's really smart, just like his older sister. She even left high school a year early to start college. Mr. Sanders called him 'Jug Head,' after he called his sister 'Nut Jar.' And Mr. Sanders warned me that Cassie is a good student, but a talker, and not to let her lead me astray."

Rose listened without interrupting, until there was a pause in Leigh's report. "Whoa, girl, take a breath," she laughed. "You can be quite a talker, too! I was hoping you'd get off to a good start, and it sure seems you did."

"Ha, I guess I was flapping my lips," she agreed. Sighing, she continued, "I'm just so glad to have met Cassie…and Les. And Alice and Cassie's cousin, Millie, seemed to get along well, too."

Alice entered the kitchen, opened the door of the ice box, and announced, "Yes, Mom, Millie and I are going to study together some if you don't mind. She lives only a couple of blocks from the school, up the hill behind the drugstore."

"Well, I'd like to meet her first before you go to her house. Why don't you invite her to come home with you some afternoon? Just let me know ahead of time, and I'll have some snacks ready for you."

"That's great! I'll ask her." Turning to grin at Leigh, Alice continued, "Mom, you know anything about fixing boys?"

"Alice, you can be such a pain in the neck!" Leigh groaned.

Rose smiled at the interaction of her daughters. "Do the boys at that school need fixing?"

"No, Mom," Alice continued taunting, "Just one in particular."

Rose laughed as Leigh moved to kick her sister's backside. "Well, what's wrong with this poor boy that he needs fixing?"

Leigh shook her head. "Oh, Mom, Alice has just got a bee in her bonnet, because Les said his best friend is really shy around girls, and Les asked me if I'd help fix him."

"Yes, Mom," added Alice, "He's really shy, but 'tall, dark, and handsome' and captain of the wrestling team."

Leigh defended herself, "Mom, I haven't even talked to the boy. I think your baby girl is the one who wants to be 'Miss Fixit.'"

Rose wiped her eyes with her apron, as she laughed at the two teenagers. "Well, neither one of you is going to be fixing any boys, at least not until after dinner. Now, both of you, get yourselves upstairs and get cleaned up." As she heard their chase ascending the stairs, she shouted: "And clean up your room—you left it in a shambles this morning."

Rose took the dinner plates from the cupboard and began setting the table in the dining room. Her daughters were such a joy to her. *What would I do without them?* she wondered. *If only Charles could realize what he's missing.* This evening, she and the girls, as usual, would sit together before the empty chair at the head of the dinner table. She appreciated Charles for providing adequately for them, though he provided abundantly for himself: tailored suits, golf club membership, and studies that added more credentials and post-nominals to his name. Rose knew he attended gatherings and dinners in his position as plant manager, but rarely did she accompany him. Even when she had, she felt out of place in her "Sunday dress" and home-permed hair, while the other wives were so stylish and professionally done-up.

But that's all a waste of time and thought, she reminded herself, as Alice bounced into the kitchen, saying, "Mom, I'll get the tea and glasses."

Leigh was close behind, adding, "And I'll get the silverware."

"Thanks, girls, hope you're hungry. I've got the pot roast and vegetables you like."

"And some of your homemade sourdough bread?" Alice asked.

"As always," Rose assured her.

Leigh placed the utensils on the table, then moved to put an arm around her mother and draw her close to confide: "Dad doesn't know what he's missing, does he, Mom?"

Rose's eyes glistened as she replied, "No, dear, and it's his loss."

Chapter 10

Hank Hodge usually stood outside Mrs. Taylor's math room at the intersection of the gym hallway and math corridor. He was allowed two minutes before the dismissal bell to arrive at his station and had an additional couple of minutes to get to his next class after the halls cleared. But, on Tuesdays and Thursdays, he was posted here during study hall, at a desk where he monitored hall passes while working on his own assignments. Hank unwrapped a piece of gum, pushed it into his mouth, returned the yellow pack to his shirt pocket, and opened the *Advanced Geometry and Trigonometry* text. He seemed to get more work done on these days without the interruptions and hum of conversations in study hall.

"Got an extra stick of that you'd be willing to give?" asked a feminine voice, as a familiar hand with rose-colored nails laid a hall pass down on his open notebook.

Hank looked up at Leigh Burkhart and cleared his throat. "Sure, here you go." He pulled the gum from his pocket and held it for her to retrieve a piece with a "Thanks a lot."

Returning the pack to his pocket, he picked up the pass and asked, "Where are you headed?"

Leigh reported, "To the office. I was told to come there during study hall to see the counselor about the transfer of my credits."

"All right." Hank checked the pass. "I see Coach signed you out." Hank returned the pass to her, and she took it from his hand with her fingertips. "Straight there and back, no side trips," he warned.

"Yes, sir, Mr. Monitor," she teased. "Thank you, sir. I sure feel safe with you on duty."

Hank grinned, "Too official?"

"Not if you're an M. P.," she shot back.

Hank laughed. "Guess I just want to make it clear I take my duty seriously."

"Well, that you do," she confirmed, as she moved toward her destination.

Hank watched Leigh's delicate form and bouncing golden hair, as she proceeded down the hallway. He felt his face burn when she waved at him over her shoulder, as if she had known his eyes were following her. He had to admit he liked this girl—she was pretty, she made him laugh, and it seemed she was beginning to enter his thoughts, even when he was supposed to be focused on other things.

Hank had closed his book bag and was re-trieving his jacket from the locker when Cassie stopped and said, "Hank, some of us are meeting down at the soda fountain. Want to join us? Les has practice, but it'd be fun to have you with us."

Hank thought for a moment and remembered his mother's warning not to be afraid. Without Les there, he likely would be the only male, unless Alex Gentry showed up. He had plenty of homework—a good reason to decline the invitation, but he'd feel like a coward if he did. "Uh, sure Cassie. I'll see you down there."

"Swell!" Cassie exclaimed. "If I'm there before you, I'll save you a chair."

"Yeah, thanks," Hank replied without enthusiasm.

The door chime sounded as Hank entered the drugstore and assessed the traffic near the soda fountain. There were a couple of tables surrounded by students and some sitting before their shakes and sodas at the bar. At one table, Cassie was seated across from Alex and Fred Gentry, with an empty chair between her and Leigh Burkhart. *This looks like a set-up*, he thought, as Cassie called out, "Over here, Hank! We saved you a place." Some irritation came with the awareness: *Les may not be here, but he's had a hand in this*.

Hank pulled the seat away from the table, placed his jacket on the back of the chair, and dropped his bookbag on the floor near the half-wall separating the soda fountain from the main store.

"Hey, Sarge, glad you could join us," Leigh announced.

Hank laughed, as Cassie asked, "What's the 'Sarge' business?"

Leigh was quick to respond, "Oh, that's a private joke."

Cassie raised a brow. "Hmm, you already have a private joke—interesting."

Changing the subject, Hank offered: "Can I get you girls some ice cream? These Gentry bums are on their own." Alex raised his cup toward Hank, and Fred chuckled.

"No, thanks, I've had a Coke," Cassie replied.

Leigh answered, "Sure, I'll take a small vanilla cone."

"What—a small? Surely, you can handle a large."

"Well, sure, bring it on!" she laughed.

Hank took change from his pocket, as he moved toward the counter and said, "Two large vanilla cones, please."

"Are you Hank?" The question came from a younger girl with brunette Shirley Temple hair and clear, pale blue eyes. She was sitting with Cassie's cousin.

"Yep, and who are you?" he responded.

"Alice Burkhart. Leigh's my older sister." She waved her cone at her friend. "Guess you know Millie."

"Sure, I've known Millie for a long time." Paying the clerk and taking the ice cream, Hank asked, "How's school going for you?"

"Oh, it's going. I like before-school and after-school better than everything in-between," she answered. "Leigh's the egg head—like my dad!"

Hank queried, "So, she's pretty smart, huh?"

"Well, nothing like your sister, so I've heard—but she's no dumb bunny!"

Hank was still laughing when he returned and handed Leigh a cone. "Your sister cracked me up. She's a cute kid."

"Thanks—the next ones will be on me," Leigh declared, saluting Hank with the proffered treat. "Well, she's mostly not a pain," Leigh agreed, "though she does about fray my last nerve sometimes."

Chuckling, Hank replied, "I only have an older sister, so I guess I'm the nerve-frayer in my family."

"So, you said you're not going to fly the coop like she did?" Leigh questioned, lounging back in her chair as she licked the ice cream.

Cassie interjected: "He can't leave us humble beings to fend for ourselves. He's 'Mr. North Side'!"

"Hardly, Cass." Hank realized he was beginning to relax. He leaned on his elbows on the table, his focus on the cone in his hand as he spoke. "No, I'm graduating. Not even sure I'll go straight to college, like Nancy. I may try to get into the Army Air Corps, especially with things looking like we may have to help deal with Hitler and his henchmen."

"So, Sarge, you're of a military mindset," Leigh observed.

Hank tilted his head a bit and considered his response. "Not so much that. But I do want to serve the country—and learning to fly would be exciting."

Alex and Fred had listened to the repartee while they polished off their milkshakes. The sucking sound from an empty cup preceded Alex's question: "What do you think, Hank—are we going to join the fight?"

"Well, the way my dad and I see it, the U. S. can't remain neutral for long. We're supplying the Allies—we're in it already in a sense. I don't think they'd have instated a peacetime draft unless the powers that be weren't figuring we'd be in it alongside them and the British, especially after what happened to the French."

"Could you guys be drafted?" Cassie was biting the inside of her lip, as she asked.

Hank knew Cassie's curiosity came from concern for Les. He answered: "We don't even have to register till we're twenty-one. That could change, but not unless the U.S. gets dragged into war."

Leigh squeezed Cassie's hand under the table and interrupted the conversation: "Okay, guys, let's leave all this war talk for another time. The soda fountain is for mindless teenage blather."

Hank thought, *Yeah, I like this girl. She's smart and kind. She's not just a strange, threatening female. She's a lot like Nut Jar.* Hank realized he no longer felt uncomfortable around Leigh—and he wanted to know more about the mind behind the pretty face.

Chapter 11

Nancy picked up her purse, leaving her open books on the library table in the quiet nook she usually frequented. She had studied more than two hours solid. She needed to take a break—go to the restroom, walk around, maybe even step outside in the sunshine for a few minutes. From her bag, she took the empty pint milk bottle she had brought for filling from the fountain located between the men's and ladies' rooms. After splashing some cold water on her face, she took the bottle outside to the front steps, where she sat on the retaining wall and closed her eyes against the gentle breeze, with only a hint of crispness on this glorious autumn day. Trees on the manicured campus lawn were almost fully adorned in their seasonal finery, and other students here and there seemed to be relishing the beauty and freedom of the hour.

"Miss Hodge, I believe it is?" The words startled her, as they rained down from above. Towering over her was the chemistry lab instructor, Jeffrey Langston.

"Oh, hello, Mr. Langston. I was just taking a break from studying—just enjoying this beautiful day."

"Yes, it is. Do you regularly study at the library?"

"Well, on Tuesdays and Thursdays, when I'm here for labs. I have several hours in the morning before our class meets. I find I can get a lot done during that time, especially here. It's quiet and seems to be conducive to all things studious," she smiled.

"Yes, it's always been my favorite place to hole up when on campus." Mr. Langston continued down the steps, then stopped at a landing. "Uh, well, Miss Hodge, I'll see you soon for lab. Enjoy the sunshine. Perhaps, we'll bump into each other here again."

"See you later, Mr. Langston," Nancy responded. She found herself curious about this obviously intelligent, seemingly shy, and oddly attractive young man. She thought it must be challenging for an academic like him to have to deal with Chem I students, most of whom were unserious about more than just checking off a B. S. requirement. She had approached her work seriously—it was necessary to her planned career, but she also wanted to do well to show Mr. Langston her appreciation for his effort—that she considered it beneficial and important.

Nancy pulled the bell to signal her intention of getting off on Frazier. She gathered her belongings, made her way to the front of the bus, then descended onto the corner adjacent the drugstore. With at least half an hour before her dad's arrival, Nancy sauntered down the block—past the barber shop, where a customer was lathered and ready for the blade; past the bakery, where she passed through a cloud of the aroma of fresh cinnamon rolls; one of the ubiquitous "five and dime" stores; a law office that, through the window, seemed all glossy dark hardwoods and green plaid upholstery; and finally, the drugstore, claiming the largest inventory of pharmaceuticals, cosmetics, and personal care items north of the river. Nancy didn't mind waiting for her dad in the comfort of the soda fountain, where she could enjoy a drink or a treat and be free of concentration on anything—just mindless wonderings and daydreams.

"Well, missy, what will you have today," inquired Betty, from behind the counter. Nancy had become such a regular, the fountain worker seemed not only friendly, but motherly.

"Oh, Miss Betty, I think I'll just have some cold chocolate milk."

"Surely, you want a little ice cream in there."

"Well...okay, sounds good. Let's make it a full-fledged milkshake."

As she filled the metal container with milk and ice cream and added a few squirts of rich, dark chocolate syrup, Betty observed: "You have to be tired after lugging all those books around all day.

You need a good old chocolate milkshake for a boost of energy."

Nancy laughed. "You sell me that way almost every school day."

"Yep, and it works, doesn't it?"

"Too easily," Nancy agreed, as she moved to sit at the counter with the loquacious waitress.

"Just curious," began Betty, "but a pretty girl like you must have a fellow to chauffeur her around at times." The blender began to whirl, and Betty churned the cup up and down, before silencing the motor, pouring the shake into a fountain glass, popping in a straw, and setting the thick treat in front of Nancy.

Nancy laughed, "I do—the handsomest you ever saw—and strong and smart and kind and just about everything you'd want in a man."

"You don't say! Tell me more, sweetie—I've got to hear about this guy."

"Well, he's picking me up here in a few minutes."

"Really? You need to introduce me."

"Well, if he comes in, I will. He usually just picks me up out front. We don't have much time before he has to get home for supper with his wife and son."

"What! Nancy, what do you mean? Surely, you aren't…"

"No, Betty, I'm just kidding you. He's my dad."

"Why, you stinker! You had me going!"

"Until I can find a man just like my dad, he'll be the only chauffeur I want."

The door chimed and Betty looked up to see a man removing his cap and smiling, as he walked toward the soda fountain. A tall, ruggedly handsome fellow, he sat on the stool next to Nancy and said to Betty, "Miss, may I have a straw, if you don't mind. This young lady is going to be fat and boyfriend-less if she keeps drinking these things by herself."

"Dad! We were just talking about you! Betty, this is my dad, Josh Hodge."

"Pleased to meet you, sir," Betty responded. "And here's your straw."

Josh took the straw and helped himself to some milkshake, then declared, "That's about the best milkshake I believe I've tasted, Miss Betty."

"Well, thank you, sir. It's all in the blending," she chuckled, then busied herself with cleaning utensils.

"Um, this is good," Josh said, taking another sip before standing. "I've got to pick up a prescription from the pharmacy. When you finish, just get your things together, and I'll meet you at the car. It's parked out front."

"Okay, Dad. You're not sick are you?" Nancy had never known her dad to need medicine for anything.

"Oh, no, just something the doctor advised I keep on hand in case of emergency." Handing her the car keys, he added: "Here, take these. I locked the doors." Before he left the soda fountain, Josh called to the waitress, "Miss Betty, thanks for the straw and the milkshake—and for keeping an eye on my girl."

She waved at Josh and said, "No problem, Mr. Hodge. You come in any time and have a straw—maybe even your own milkshake," she laughed and agreed, "And your Nancy is a sweet-heart!"

He replied, "Yes, ma'am, that she is…that she is."

Chapter 12

"Okay, Hank, spot me on the bench," Les said, as he adjusted the iron weight disks and dried his hands. "I'm going up to five sets, but I'm nearly fatigued already. Got to get more rest. Spent too much time with Cass last night."

Les reclined on the bench and huffed as he pumped the iron bar with eighty pounds on each end.

"You're going light today," Hank observed.

Les finished the last set of ten and returned the bar to the rack without assistance. "Well, like I said, I'm tired. I'm going to rest up some this off week." Les sat up and reached for the towel Hank offered. "We had a long practice this morning. But, when Coach said he'd be here this afternoon and would open the weight room, I felt like I ought to take the opportunity."

Hank sat cross-legged on the nearby mat and said, "So, you and Cassie had a late date last night?"

Hank wiped his face and admitted, "Well, not so much a date as a planning session," Les chuckled. We sat on her front porch and talked until after midnight."

"I can't imagine having that much to say to any girl!"

Les held the towel next to the hairline, drip-ping sweat into his ear. "Cassie's not just any girl, my friend. I'm going to marry her."

"And you're sure about that? She's got an-other whole year till she graduates."

"Hank, I'm absolutely sure. I love her. I'll wait for her to grow up a bit more—grow up some more myself. But we're going to have a life together."

Hank stood and picked fifteen-pound dumb-bells from the rack. He puffed through curls, "How do you know?"

Les had begun wiping down the equipment with disinfectant, as he replied, "Know what?"

"Know you love her ... know you're going to marry her?"

Les stopped, seeming to give serious thought to his reply: "Well, nobody knows for sure what the future holds. But I know I love her, because I know thinking about any future without her gives me a lit-eral pain in my solar plexus!" He laughed as he added, "Maybe one of these days, Junior Buddy, you'll know what I mean."

Hank's biceps kept flexing, one after the other, as he wandered away in thought.

Les finished his clean up and stored the cleaner away in the nearby cabinet. Noticing Hank, he said, "Hey, bud. Hank!"

"Oh, yeah, Les, what'd you say?"

"Well, I didn't really say anything, but you're giving your biceps a beating."

"Oh, yeah, I guess I forgot to count."

"You've got some deep thoughts going on in there," Les laughed, smacking Hank on the back of the head with his towel.

Hank grinned and put the dumbbells back in the rack.

"You got something bugging you?" Les inquired. "You know, you can talk to me. And, of course, I am older, wiser, and more experienced," he chuckled.

"No, nothing's really bugging me. Guess I just can't get this girl thing figured out."

"What's to figure … besides their figures?" Les joked, raising his eyebrows and whistling low.

"Yeah, right. Well, you know there's more to it than that." Hank moved to a wrestling mat and sat down again, leaning against the concrete wall. Les stationed himself on the weight bench.

"What do you mean?"

"Well, you say you're going to marry Cassie. There has to be more than just a girl's face and figure. Lots of girls are pretty—but you know they may not stay pretty forever. What is it about Cassie that makes you love her enough to want to spend all your life with her?"

"Whoa, we're getting deep today, aren't we?" Les considered his response, then said, "Well … she makes me smile. Even when I'm down for some reason—like that "D" I made on that English paper last spring, or worse, losing to Grandview last season—even then, she made me feel it was all right—nothing knocked me down in her eyes."

Hank studied the nails of his clenched hands, as he listened and waited without speaking for Les to continue: "And she's honest without ever being unkind. She's cute and bouncy, but she's also tough and courageous. Ha, she's nearly a foot shorter, but she knows how to keep me at arm's length, if I get too cozy."

In a momentary silence, Hank looked up to see Les pressing the towel to his eyes, before he continued: "Guess what it boils down to, I trust her—I trust her to love me, in good times and not so good times, and I trust her to be the mother of my kids someday. And she knows she can trust me."

Hank was reminded of Mr. Sanders' reading: "It was the best of times, it was the worst of times …" He stood up from the mat and said simply, "Thanks, Les."

"No problem, Junior Bud," Les quipped, "I'd rather have you come to me than see your name show up in the 'Advice to the Lovelorn' column—not that I read it, of course—just kidding."

They were walking out of the weight room and across the sideline of the football field, when Hank blurted out the question that had broken through the restraint of timidity: "Les, how do I go about asking Leigh for a date?"

"What?" Les slapped Hank on the back. "Well, hot diggity! I thought the day would never come! You're ready to expand your comfort zone and join the world of two sexes!"

Hank laughed and flushed with embarrassment. "She seems like a nice girl. I'm pretty relaxed around her. I just thought I might try to get to know her better."

Les thought for a moment, then said, "Tell you what—I'll talk to Cassie. Maybe we can arrange a double date, maybe go out after the next game, or maybe take in a movie at the Tivoli. I think everything would be smoother for you if we were all together. If you two really hit it off, you can take it from there—fly solo if you want."

Hank felt the tension flowing from him at the suggestion. "Les, man, that would be great. Really, thanks. Just let me know what you work out and when I should ask her. It'll be a lot easier for me—and for her, too, I bet, if she knows we'll be with you and Cassie."

River Sisters, the Strangers

Les put his arm around Hank's shoulders. "No, problem, junior, your senior bud is here to guide and advise."

Chapter 13

Sunday was the day of worship for the Hodge family, and Nancy always enjoyed the fellowship of the congregants and the exuberance of the children, running around the enclosed yard at the rear of the building, joyful that parents had stayed after the service to talk with church family and visitors. Nancy always left morning worship, especially on a beautiful blue-sky day like today, feeling renewed, hopeful, even abundantly loved by good people, who had known and encouraged her since she, too, was running around the grassy playground.

She was leaning against the family car watching the boisterous activity of the children, when Hank joined her and leaned next to her against the maroon sedan. "Hey, Nut Jar, wishing you could be in there with them?"

"Just having sweet memories, no longings to return. I'm at a point where I don't like my dresses dirty and my knees skinned," she laughed. "What about you?"

"Oh, I'm just minding my manners—and our mother. If I gave into my inner child, I'd probably be right in the middle of the action."

Nancy smiled at Hank, aware he was becoming quite a handsome and mature young man. "Are Mom and Dad on their way?"

"Dad's got a short meeting, and Mom's talking to a couple of ladies about the potluck coming up. They may be a few minutes."

"Well, how's school going? We haven't talked much lately. I think my nose is actually shorter from having it crammed in a book, hours on end every day."

"All my classes are good. Grades are holding up."

"How are Les and Cassie?"

"Oh, they're great." Hank paused. "Les seems sure marriage is in their not-too-distant future."

"Hmm, interesting." Nancy glanced sideway at her brother to sense his reaction as she said, "Don't guess you've got anyone on the horizon yet."

"No, not really," he admitted, "but there is a girl who might double-date with me and Cassie and Les."

"You don't say!" Nancy exclaimed. "Well, this must be quite a girl to get your attention."

"She is easy on the eyes," he said, elbowing his sister. "But she's a good student, not flashy or flirty, I think. Kind of straight-forward, not timid."

Jan Dearman

"Well, I know it's not all that important, but what does she look like—blonde, brunette, red-head...bald?"

"Bald, actually, how'd you guess? And her front two teeth are missing, but the rest seem mostly solid and white. Her eyes are really big and blue, especially through those half-inch lenses she wears." Nancy cackled with laughter that doubled in volume when Hank added, "She's kind of skinny, but she says the vitamin shots she's taking should get her up to eighty pounds in a few months. Her feet won't look quite so big then."

Nancy tried to compose herself, commanding, "Hank, hush, you idjit! Be serious!"

Hank handed her the handkerchief from his pocket. She wiped the tears from her eyes, knowing nothing gave Hank more pleasure than to make her lose complete control with his humor.

Nancy sniffed, "All right, now give me the real low-down on this girl—name, approximate height and weight, hair, eyes, et cetera, et cetera."

"You sound like you're filling out a patient's medical information!"

"Hank, I mean it—seriously."

"Okay, Sis. Well, she is about your height—maybe a bit curvier in the right places, if you get my drift." Nancy, grinning, elbowed him. "Ouch! No need to get violent!" He continued: "She has long

73

wavy blonde hair, about down to here." He gestured to the top of his shoulder. "She has these blue-gray eyes that look silvery in the sunlight. Her teeth are pearly whites, none apparently missing. And, last but not least, if anything, her feet are on the smallish side."

Nancy pursued more information. "And you say she's a good student?"

"I have heard from a most reliable source, she is not on a par with you, but 'she is no dumb bunny.' I believe those were the exact words."

"And who would this reliable source be?" Nancy queried.

"Her occasionally nerve-fraying kid sister, and your nerve-fraying kid brother has all confidence in a fellow younger sibling."

"'Nerve-fraying'—that's a useful description. I'll keep it in store for future reference. Well, what's her name, what's her sister's name, and when is this double-date to take place?"

"Leigh—Leigh Burkhart. Younger sister, Alice. Double date, don't know. I haven't asked her yet. I'm waiting for Les to get back to me about some options for when and where."

"Are you prepared to ask her out? Not nervous?"

"No, and yes, I'm nervous. But she doesn't make me as uncomfortable as some girls do. She's

74

Jan Dearman

easy-going, friendly, more like a guy, I guess—or like you."

Nancy cackled again, this time that Hank was so oblivious to the funniness of his description: a seemingly beautiful girl he found attractive because she was "more like a guy" or like his sister. "Hank Hodge, I look forward to meeting this girl. She sounds like one-of-a kind!"

"Sorry to hold you up, children. I know you're probably hungry and tired of waiting," Eliza declared as she and Josh approached the vehicle.

"Oh, Mom, you just don't know," Nancy replied. "I've been laughing too hard to hear my stomach growling."

"Well, son, I guess you've been keeping your sister entertained," Josh added. "Maybe you can review the show for us after dinner."

"Well, Dad," Hank teased, "I think I'm only good for one performance today." He got Nancy's attention, winked at her, and put his finger to his lips to caution her to silence.

75

Chapter 14

Seeing a sliver of light at the bottom of the door to her parents' room, Leigh knocked. She knew her mother was awake, likely sitting in the armchair by the window, reading or working crossword puzzles under the light of the nearby pole lamp. Never one to complain or argue, her mother usually waited this way for Charles Burkhart to come home, often into late hours that left her drained of energy and any remnant of hope for a pleasant homecoming.

"Come in, dear."

"Mom, can I bother you for a bit?" Leigh inquired.

"Oh, precious, you know you are never a bother." Rose laid the puzzle and pencil on the tray of the pole lamp and motioned for her daughter to come sit in front of her and, as she often did, to lay her head in her mother's lap. Rose combed the wavy blonde tresses with her fingers and asked, "Everything going well with you?"

"Mom, there's this boy—the one that needs fixing," she giggled with her mother. "Cassie said he's going to ask me out, on a double date with her and Les." Leigh waited for her mother's response.

"Well, Leigh, I see no problem with that. From what little I know, he sounds like a good boy, and Cassie and Les will be with you. You are nearly seventeen. What are you planning to do on this double-date?"

Leigh recounted the information Cassie had given her, adding, "It might be a late night, since it's after the game—maybe 11:30."

"That doesn't sound unreasonable. Of course, you must be where you say you're going to be—and be back by 11:30."

"Thanks, Mom. Of course, Hank hasn't even asked me yet. He's never asked anybody for a date, and Cassie said she and Les were wondering if he'll have the nerve to follow through."

Rose smiled, as she said, "Well, sounds to me like this will be a momentous occasion. And aren't you the honored one—the first girl to be asked out by the president of the Student Council and the captain of the wrestling team!"

"There'll be no dates with anyone," Charles Burkhart declared, entering the room.

Leigh stood, as her mother rose from the chair. "Charles, you're home early. Can I fix you some dinner? There are leftovers …"

"No, I've eaten, and don't change the subject. She's not going to date one of the boys around here, not while she's living under this roof."

"Charles, she's almost seventeen, and this boy is a fine student and a gentleman."

"Shut up, Rose. I said no and that's final."

Leigh felt anger and indignation burning through her reason. "You shouldn't talk to Mother that way. She waits up for you to come home night after night—sometimes falls asleep in that chair and doesn't wake up until morning. You have no right to talk to her like that, or to have any say in my life!"

Leigh was making her way past Charles to leave the room, when he grabbed her arm, pulled her toward him, and slapped the side of her face. "You'll not disrespect me!" he blared.

"Charles, no!" Rose pulled his arm away from Leigh. "Leave her alone, please!" The back of the same arm swung at Rose and knocked her to the floor against the chair.

Feeling the sting of her cheek, but refusing to allow tears to escape her eyes, Leigh went to her mother and helped her to her feet. "Are you all right, Mom?"

"Yes, dear, go on to your room. I'll handle this."

"No, Mother, I've had enough!" Leigh positioned herself in front of her father: "You can slap me again if you like, but if I ever see you lay a hand on Mother again, you'll be sorry. I'll march myself down to that fancy office of yours and tell all your high-class friends and doting employees that you beat up on your wife and daughter. Of course, that's only on the rare occasion you come home. I'm sure the other women in your life would find it hard to believe you're such a bully."

"They'd never believe...don't you dare..." Charles stammered.

Leigh interrupted him: "Oh, yes, I'll dare. And I'll have the bruises to prove it." Leigh pulled up the sleeve of her sweater to reveal the old yellow discolorations and the fresh contusions on her forearm. Turning to her mother, she asked, "Mom, you okay?"

"Yes, Leigh. Go on, dear."

Leigh moved toward the door, but Charles pushed her out of the way as he made an exit. His footsteps sounded on the stairs, the front door slammed, and soon the car engine roared.

Leigh returned to Rose, now sitting again in the chair. Tears glistened on her mother's cheeks. "Leigh, I'm so sorry. This is all my fault. I'm just so sorry," she sobbed.

Leigh's tears flowed with her mother's. "No, Mom, it's not your fault. You've done nothing wrong. He's a bitter, angry man, who can't seem to find happiness in his own home—and won't let us be happy when he's in it."

Leigh was quiet the next morning, as she prepared for the last day of the school week. Alice, as usual, was sleepy and cranky about her "hand-me-down" dress—a pink skirt with a pink and blue floral top with puffed sleeves. Alice said it made her "look like a six-year-old." Leigh was just thankful her younger sister slept like the dead and didn't hear the tumult of the previous night. Leigh covered the purple bruises on her arm with a long-sleeved blue pullover, worn over her white blouse. She was thankful there was an early fall chill in the air and hopeful the sweater would not be too warm for comfort before the end of the school day. The heavy class ring on her father's hand had left a bruise on her cheek, but with her hair down and fluffed out, it was hardly noticeable.

As the girls entered the kitchen, Rose was closing their lunch bags. To Leigh, it seemed her mother avoided eye contact as she chirped as usual, "Good morning, girls. There are blueberry muffins and juice on the table. We're running a bit late this morning, so no time to dawdle."

Leigh sat at the table, considered the muffins, and said, "Think I'll just have some juice, Mom. Maybe have a muffin for a snack after school."

Alice wolfed down a second muffin and gulped her juice, before picking up her lunch bag and declaring, "Love you, Mom. I'm gone—got to meet Millie and compare our algebra homework before school—see if we got the same answers."

"Hold on, Alice, I'm going with you." Leigh picked up her lunch bag, then moved toward Rose, grasped her mother's arm, and made her turn to look into her eyes. "I'll let you know how the day goes. I'm okay, Mom, and you're going to be okay too. Just remember, he's a bully. He'll be a bully until you stand up for yourself." Leigh saw tears pool in the corner of her mother's eyes as she nodded softly, and Leigh kissed her mother's cheek.

Chapter 15

Friday study halls always seemed to buzz with muted conversations, occasional outbursts of giggles, and an occasional warning from Coach Leonard: "Students, tone it down! You're getting too noisy." Usually Hank would be irritated by the interference with study time that he hoped would reduce his weekend homework. But … today was the day he would ask Leigh to double with him, Cassie, and Les, after the game next Friday. Hank wondered if Cassie had said anything to Leigh and, if she had, what Leigh was thinking about the plan. Les said his dad had agreed to let them use the '35 Chevy sedan he and his dad kept polished and fine-tuned. After the anticipated post-game celebration on the field, Les would shower and dress, and they would go over the river to the Dynamo Diner, known for "the biggest and best burgers in the Dynamo City," along with a juke box that played the latest hits.

Only the evening before, at the family dinner table, Hank had approached his parents about the proposed double-date and their potential approval or disapproval. Nancy started giggling when her dad stopped, fork not all the way to his mouth, and stared at his son, who had just blurted: "Dad, Mom, uh, I'm going to ask Leigh Burkhart to double-date with me and Cassie and Les, if y'all don't mind."

Eliza immediately covered for Josh and said, "Why, son...I think that's a fine idea. You're a junior now, and it's high time for you to start getting out and having fun with your friends. Don't you think so, Josh?"

"Uh, well, yes, I guess that's right," Josh admitted. "I think I was just caught a bit off-guard. Sure, son, just mind your manners. Be a gentleman. Les seems to be a good boy and a safe driver. Just don't get into any kind of trouble."

"Oh, Josh, you know your son. You can trust him always to be a fine young Christian man," Eliza declared.

Josh frowned a bit and inquired: "Do I know this girl? Who is she?"

Nancy, gleeful, interjected: "She's bald and skinny, with big blue eyes, when seen through her thick lenses, and her feet look kind of big, but it's just because she's so skinny. But she's taking growth vitamins." Hank started laughing at his sister's reiteration of the description, and they all guffawed when Eliza said, "See, Josh, he's a good and kind boy. He takes pity on the impaired."

Reliving the humor of the previous evening, Hank grinned as left his post and made his way to study hall. The whole "revealing" to his parents and their reaction seemed to give him new courage, even an easiness, to approach Leigh. In recent study hall periods, she had managed to have an empty desk nearby when he entered from hall monitor duty, and today there was one just to her left. *Perfect*, he thought, as he sat in the chair and dropped his book bag on the floor.

Leigh sat with her elbow on the desktop and her face in her hand. She casually observed: "Well, don't you look like the cat that swallowed the canary—grinning ear to ear!"

"Oh, was I? Guess I was … well, just thinking about something funny my sister said."

"You mean, she's smart and funny?"

"Yep," he joked, "can you believe it? A lot like you, I bet."

"Oh, yeah, I try to hide my intelligence—don't want to intimidate you!"

"Me? I'm unintimidatable, don't you know?"

"Oh, really? Can you say that three times without messing up?"

They laughed, and Coach Leonard warned: "Okay, keep it down to Friday volume."

Hank gave a brief salute to Coach, signaling they'd comply. Then, he forged on with the words he had practiced: "Hey, Leigh, if you don't have any plans next Friday after the game…"

"Oh, yeah," she interrupted, "Cassie said we're all four going over to the Dynamo after the game. That sounds like lots of fun. I'm looking forward to it." She ran her fingers through her hair and pulled it over her shoulder.

Hank was perplexed. Why had he worried and planned and sweated over this whole deal? It was so easy—Leigh had made it easy. She made him feel comfortable and, somehow, more secure with … everything, even with himself.

"Hey, you've stopped grinning and gone to frowning. You okay?" she asked.

"Oh, was I?" Hank realized his concentration was not only on the awareness of new feelings, but on Leigh's silver eyes and the way her hair curved around her chin. Without thinking, he reached out and swept the tress away from her face, revealing the evidence of her father's hard hand.

"Leigh, what happened?"

Pulling away, she said, "Oh, that's just a little bruise I got running into the door at home. It's nothing."

"So, you're smart, funny, and clumsy?" he joked through his concern.

"Well, yes, a little lacking in grace and coordination. I can fall over my own feet."

Hank offered: "Maybe I can be around to lend a hand—or catch you on the way down."

River Sisters, the Strangers

Hank suspected he loved this girl when she smiled and said softly, "Yes, I'd like that."

Chapter 16

Monday afternoon of game week, Hank sat with Cassie and Leigh, Alice and Millie, around the drugstore table, where Hank had celebrated his new relationship, at least in his own mind, with a round of ice cream for everyone. He entertained the girls with the account of his bogus description of Leigh to his sister and how she had passed that on to his parents—and his mom's comic praising of his benevolent spirit. He realized he enjoyed being the instigator and focus of their giggles. "So, see," he declared, "the ice cream has to be my treat because I am so benevolent to the impaired—like you frail and fragile females." Then he added, "Especially the clumsy ones," and leaned his shoulder against Leigh.

"Watch it, bud! I'll kick you with one of these big feet of mine!" she retorted.

Hank laughed at his spontaneous idea and suggested to Leigh: "Hey, you know Halloween is coming up. We ought to get you girls over to our house, so Leigh can meet Mom and Dad. She can get some thick glasses and big shoes—whatever, to look the part, and meet the Hodges. Ha, that sounds like a radio program, 'Meet the Hodges'!" Hank licked his ice cream and added nonchalantly, "Of course, the 'skinny' part you can't pull off!"

"Why, Hank Hodge, you have no benevolent spirit for sturdy women?" Leigh chided.

Hank's comeback was quick: "Stout women like yourself don't need benevolence, just plenty of space." He joined in the guffaws of the girls, then noticed they drew the attention of customers at the pharmacy window on the other side of the store. Trying to shush them, he warned, "We're going to get thrown out of here if you silly females don't control yourselves."

Cassie responded, "You're bonkers! You're the one we stout women are going to throw out, just so we can have more space and clear the air, you goof."

"Well, sorry to leave such entertaining company," Leigh interjected, scooting her chair away from the table and standing to pick up her bag. "I told Mom we'd be home a little earlier today."

"Yeah," agreed Cassie. "I've got a lot of homework, and I need to finish it, in case Les is able to come by later. I told my mother I'd bake the cookies to have on hand if he does—he's good for nearly a dozen all by himself."

"He must be on his best behavior then," Hank informed. "I've seen him polish off nearly two dozen."

Hank held the door while the girls exited the drugstore. Leigh, the last to clear the portal, said,

"Why, thank you, sir. You are a gentleman and a scholar."

"Only living up to my mother's instruction," he quipped.

Cassie said, "See you tomorrow," as she and Millie began their walk up the hill to their neighborhood.

Hank walked with Leigh and Alice to the corner at the crosswalk and suggested, "Could I walk you girls home?"

Alice giggled when Leigh thought for a moment, then responded, "Sure, that would be nice. But don't you have to get home yourself?"

"Oh, Mom just expects me to be there in time to wash up before dinner. She won't be concerned."

Alice huffed, "We're only about three blocks from here," then added, "Maybe you can meet our mother. I look like her—we're not stout like Leigh," she teased.

Leigh sighed and looked at Hank, "See, nerve-fraying, like I said!"

"Good job, kid," he directed at Alice, "from one nerve-frayer to another."

Leigh and Alice preceded Hank through the front door of the Burkhart home, and he lingered in the small entry way while they sought their mother. He heard muffled voices, as he looked around and noticed the neat, seemingly unused living room, unlike the one he knew in the Hodge home. There were no family pictures, no stacks of books on the coffee table, no chess set like the one they left out last night in anticipation of the match this evening. To the left of a plush gray armchair and matching ottoman stood a radio receiver similar to that of the Hodges, but on a side table to the right, rested only a pipe rack and match box, obviously belonging to Mr. Burkhart. Josh thought about his father's similar burgundy lounging chair and foot stool, but on the table next to his dad's was a well-worn Bible stuffed with note papers.

Rose Burkhart, with Leigh and Alice trailing behind her, entered the hallway and extended her hand. "Hank, I'm Rose Burkhart. I'm so pleased to meet you!"

Hank saw the motherly version of an adult Alice and replied, "Same here, Mrs. Burkhart. I hope you don't mind I walked the girls home."

"Oh, no, no, I appreciate your consideration. Could I interest you in a piece of apple pie and cold milk, or would that spoil your mother's dinner?"

Standing behind her mother's shoulder, Leigh smiled and nodded encouragement, and Hank said, "Well, that sounds really good, Mrs. Burkhart. I don't know that anything has ever spoiled my appetite."

Alice, who had positioned herself on the bottom stair step to lean on the newel, excitedly turned and took her giggles up to the bedroom, crying after her, "Save a piece for me!"

The kitchen of the Burkhart home was cheery and warm, like his mother's, filled with the smell of freshly baked pie and what Hank thought was boiled ham dinner cooking in a Dutch oven on the stove.

Leigh motioned for Hank to sit at the table in the nook just past the back door, where bench seating wrapped the right angle of the corner. Hank slid onto the red vinyl-covered bench on one side of the table, and Leigh sat across from him. Rose set two glasses of milk in front of them with a generous slab of pie for Hank and napkins.

"None for me, Mom," Leigh advised. "I'll save mine for after dinner."

"Well, if you're sure." Rose brought a cane-back chair from the opposite corner of the kitchen, set it before them, and then brought a slice of pie for herself. "I'm sure Hank doesn't want to eat alone," she smiled, as she helped herself to Leigh's milk.

"Mrs. Burkhart, this is great apple pie!" Hank declared, before washing down a large bite with milk. "Mom makes really good apple pie, too, but this is a little different."

"Well, I add just a dash of nutmeg in the filling and a tablespoon of vinegar in the crust dough.

Those are the only ingredients that might be a bit different."

"Um, I'll tell her. She might want to try that." Hank wiped his mouth, then spoke.

"Mrs. Burkhart, I hope you won't mind, but I have asked Leigh to double-date with me and Les and Cassidy Friday night after the game. Les is driving his dad's car, and we're planning on going to the Dynamo Diner for hamburgers. If you would like to meet Les and Cassie before giving your approval, they'd be happy to drop by after school one day this week."

"Well, Hank, I really appreciate your coming by to talk to me about your plans. I assume Leigh agrees," Rose teased, smiling at her daughter. "I have no problem with your double-date. I trust Leigh and her choice of friends. Just be where you say you're going to be, and have Leigh home by 11:30, if possible. If you're delayed for some reason, try to find a phone and give me a call. I'll be up."

"Yes, ma'am, I will—and I'll take good care of Leigh," Hank promised.

Leigh added, "Thanks, Mom, but try to get some sleep while you wait. I'll make sure I let you know I'm home."

"That'll be fine." Turning to Hank, Rose asked, "How about another piece of pie?"

Hank laughed, "Oh, no, ma'am. That just might interfere with Mom's dinner. But I sure did enjoy it." Hank scooted from the bench, as he said, "Well, I don't mean to eat and run, but I'd better start home."

"Do you live far from here?" Rose asked.

"Well, probably about five miles," he laughed.

"Five miles!" Rose exclaimed. "Do you walk to and from school every day?"

"Oh, no, ma'am. My dad brings me in the morning, and I can ride the school bus most days. But Mom knows I'm a threat to walk home on a nice day—sometimes even run, if I don't have books to carry. And when I have wrestling practice after school, Dad usually picks me up."

"Well, then, you'd better go along." Rose and Leigh followed Hank to the front door.

"I do appreciate your seeing the girls home. I hope you'll come again when you can stay longer and visit."

"Thanks, Mrs. Burkhart. See you tomorrow, Leigh." He winked at Mrs. Burkhart and added, calling up the stairs, "Hey, fellow nerve-frayer, see you around!" They all laughed to hear Alice's unrestrained giggles, coming from her position within earshot. Then Hank exited to the porch and waved before the door closed and he proceeded down the steps.

He hardly had reached the street when a gray Chevrolet sedan turned into the Burkhart driveway. Hank noticed the car slowed, and the driver turned to scowl at him briefly before pulling toward the house and turning off the engine. Assuming Mr. Burkhart had arrived home early, Hank was thankful he had made a timely departure. Leigh's father seemed disturbed to see a strange boy in his yard, and Hank wondered what he would think about the upcoming date.

Chapter 17

The Dynamo Diner was alive with boisterous Friday night high school football post-game celebrations and, in some cases, muted consolation get-togethers with post-mortems of their losses. Les and Cassie led Hank and Leigh to their customary corner booth that a friendly waiter always tried to hold for Les on game nights, until the boss ordered, "Let it go." The four ran a gauntlet of "Good game, Les!" and "Way to go, Northside!" exclamations—even a few "We'll be back, Thompson!" threats. Les, reserved, gave a two-finger salute to acknowledge the attention, while making his way doggedly to the relative seclusion of the booth.

The waiter met them as they settled onto the benches: "Hey, Les! Congratulations on the game! Can I get the usual for you and Cass?"

"Thanks, Vic," Les replied, "Yep, for Cassie and me. What are you two going to have?" he directed to Hank.

Turning to Leigh, Hank questioned: "What'll you have—burger and fries? A Coke?"

"Sure," Leigh answered, "Sounds good."

"Same all around," Les concluded. "Thanks, Vic."

"No problem. Back in a snap with your drinks." The waiter left their table to enter the nearby hallway leading to the kitchen.

"Whew," sighed Les, stretching and rubbing his shoulder. "I'm glad that game's over. It feels good to come out on top, but I think the mental stress wears me out sometimes more than the physical," he admitted.

"Well, you've got, what, five more games till the playoff?" asked Hank.

"Yeah. And the more we win, the harder the pressure to keep the streak going."

Cassie interjected: "You can do it. You're the key player. What do they say, 'The greater the ability, the greater the responsibility'?" She placed her hand on his arm and said, "I'm proud of you, Les."

"Well," he grinned, placing his hand over Cassie's, "that's real motivation, coming from my girl!" Les continued, asking Hank, "How's the wrestling season looking?"

"We're in good shape, I think. Mostly experienced wrestlers back this year, and the new guys are strong and coachable."

"Oh, listen!" Leigh interjected. "Chattanooga Choo-Choo!"

The four nodded to the swing beat, and Les played percussion with his fingers on the table, as the four listened to the popular Glenn Miller tune. They joined in singing, "Chattanooga Choo Choo, won't you choo-choo me home?"

"We've got to see that movie!" Les declared. "It was canceled during the polio shut-down, but the Tivoli's going to run it again starting Sunday. Maybe we could all get-together and go to the matinee." Directing his remark to Hank, Les continued: "The movie is less than a couple of hours long. I'd have you back in time to meet your family for the evening service."

Hank replied, "Why don't you all just plan to come back to my house for some sandwiches. Then you all meet with us Sunday evening, and afterward we can get some ice cream at the Castle."

"That would be swell!" came Cassie's enthusiastic response.

"Well, I'll have to check with my mother," answered Leigh, "but I don't think she'll mind. Maybe you could call me tomorrow, and I can let you know."

"Sure thing," Hank answered. "I'll call you before lunch—or are you up by then?"

Leigh teased, "Well, even if I'm not, I'll drag myself out of the bed just to answer the phone." Then she continued, "Of course, I'll be up, silly! You don't think I'm some kind of ritzy lady of leisure, do you?"

Hank put his arm around Leigh's shoulders. "I guess you just look like a lady of leisure," he said, before adding with a grin, "who needs her beauty sleep."

Leigh laughed and directed her question to the group: "Can anyone tell me how I should take that comment?"

They all laughed when Les explained, "Oh, I think Hank meant to say, 'who *gets* lots of beauty sleep,'" then, directed to Hank, "You got to watch your use of verbs, Junior Bud!"

Imitating the Virginia dialect of their junior English teacher, Cassie intoned: "Mr. Hodge, you must clarify the connotation of the compliment you wish to convey."

Hank chuckled: "Okay, Leigh. You look well-rested and as my Aunt Lindy says, 'cute as a little pink pig'!"

Leigh feigned insult, as she responded, "Oh, so now I'm lazy and porky! I feel so flattered—or should I say 'fattered'!"

Les stopped the car at the end of the Burkharts' walkway and, with Cass, waited for Hank to escort Leigh to her front door.

Hank noted on his watch they had beat the curfew by almost ten minutes, before he said, "Leigh, I had a swell time tonight. Please tell your mother 'Thanks' again from me for letting you go. And remember, I'll call you tomorrow to find out about Sunday and the movie and all."

"I had a swell time, too, Hank—lots of fun. I look forward to Sunday, and I'll get up early— maybe 10:30 or 11:00," she teased, "just to get your call."

"Well," Hank hesitated, "I'd better get going. Les has to get Cassie home."

He had turned to leave when Leigh said, "Wait, Hank." She crossed the short space between them to kiss him on the cheek and say, "Thanks, Hank. Really, thanks a lot."

Hank watched her as she entered and turned to wave, before closing the door on the first day of what he knew would be the remainder of a life he wanted to share with no one but Leigh Burkhart. This was such a sudden realization, a new enlighten-ment—love—a "one and only," who made him feel alive and whole, with whom life's blessings would be sweeter and who would make nothing the world threw at him insurmountable. In the span of one brief date, with one simple, sweet kiss on the cheek, before he reached the waiting car, Hank had formulated a dream, a purpose, and a goal—not only to get himself successfully through this life to the next, but to make Leigh Burkhart the partner by his side, all the way. Remembering Mr. Sanders' reading, Hank thought, *This must be the best of times.*

Chapter 18

"Charles, Leigh is going to a movie tomorrow with Les, Cassie, and Hank," Rose declared, wiping her hands on the dish towel with which she had just dried the breakfast dishes. "I thought you ought to know."

Charles Burkhart looked up from his paper to ask, "And that should interest me for what reason?"

"Well, I thought you might want to meet Hank—perhaps, all three of her friends. They are good students—good people. Hank will be coming tomorrow afternoon to pick her up."

Her husband folded the paper and laid it in his lap, before reaching for the Meerschaum from the nearby pipe rack. "You and Leigh are responsible for all this—and for whatever mischief comes from her relationship with one of these boys." He tamped down the tobacco, lit a match, and drew on the pipe to draw the flame down into the bowl. He continued, "But don't get any ideas that Alice will follow Leigh's example. She'll be going back home to settle down when the time comes."

"Charles, why did you move us down here? You knew the girls would be in school here and would meet Southern boys they might marry some-day."

"The promotion, of course. Why else? And, as for marriage, they will follow my direction—at least Alice will," he added with a huff. "You and Leigh can do what you will with her life, but Alice will do as I say." Holding the pipe between his teeth, he opened the paper again, erecting a barrier to further communication.

Rose retreated to the kitchen nook, where she sat with her cup containing the final remains of the morning's coffee—strong, dark, and as bitter as the thoughts whirling in her mind. At least Charles seemed resigned to shutting Leigh out of his realm of control, and Leigh had made it clear he was to stay more than an arm's length away from her. But Rose knew she must somehow keep Alice safe, build some protection around her, without confrontation or conflict with Charles—and, prayerfully, without his revealing what she assumed to be the source of his vexed and overbearing nature. She sometimes wondered if knowing the truth about her real father would make Leigh's life easier—at least, give Leigh some explanation for the emotional, sometimes physical abuse she had suffered. But Rose believed herself a coward to move so quickly into the arms of a man she didn't really know, to place the welfare of her child in his hands. Now, she was afraid to reveal the truth to that child, for fear of losing her love and respect in the knowledge of her mother's fearful dependency. Thankfully, it seemed, Leigh had Jack's bravery, and Rose realized she herself was holding onto the coattails of Leigh's courage.

Chapter 19
October 1941

"Whew! All that snow and ice gave me a chill," Cassie exclaimed, as they made their way up the aisle to the elegant foyer of the theater.

Les threw his jacket around her shoulders. "Here, maybe this will help."

"That Sonja Henie is a cute little cookie, isn't she?" observed Leigh. "They say she couldn't even speak English when she made her first movie."

"Looks like she's got a handle on it, now," Hank said. "What'd you think of the Tivoli?"

"Oh, it's beautiful! I can just envision Scarlett descending down that grand staircase!" Leigh noted, as they passed under the ornate foyer of the upper level, approached via a galley with wings of steps curving down to the polished white marble floors of the first floor. "Everything about it is just so…well, grand!"

Cassie said, "Thank you, guys. The movie was swell, and the company was even better." She smiled at Les and took his hand, as they walked toward the parked car.

"Yes," agreed Leigh. "It has been such a great date! Thanks so much."

"Ours has been the pleasure," responded Les. "We've got two dishy dames at our sides. Ain't we the lucky guys!"

They laughed as they strolled up Broad Street behind Les and Cass. Leigh held Hank's arm, and he put his hand over hers. "This is nice," he said. "Just you and me, on a beautiful October day, not a care in the world."

Leigh laughed, "Well, just you and me and Cassie and Les."

"Oh, they're in their own little world," Hank chuckled, "and we can be in one of our own making."

As Les pulled out of the parking space to begin his approach to the bridge, Hank asked: "You girls still agreeable to hanging out at my house for an hour or so?"

"Sure," said Cassie.

"Looking forward to meeting your mom and dad—and Nut Jar," Leigh laughed.

Les added, "Well, I'm looking forward to a big banana split this evening."

"That'll be great," Leigh responded, "as long as it's not too late an evening. Guess who's got three pages to write before English class tomorrow?"

"Uh-oh, never would have figured you for a procrastinator," observed Hank.

Leigh gave him a playful punch and said, "Well, I've had other things on my mind this week-end—like you, you knucklehead."

"Oh, really?" Hank replied. "Well, I managed to get my paper written—oh, wait, that was a letter to you."

"Should I be looking for that to arrive in the mail this week?" she teased.

"Hmm, no, better look for it under your usual desk in study hall. Not sure I can afford a stamp after tonight." Noticing Leigh's silent, questioning expression, he laughed and said, "I'm just kidding!"

They all guffawed at the reprimand from Les: "Junior Buddy, you've still got a lot to learn about women!"

Hank opened the door to usher his friends into the wide center hallway. "Hey, Mom! Got a crew here to see you!"

Eliza Hodge emerged from the kitchen door-way, wiping her hands on the blue-checked pinafore apron tied over the white blouse tucked into her navy suit skirt. She still wore the comfortable gray, fur-lined house slippers, for which she had swapped black leather pumps as soon as she had returned home after morning worship. "Why, Les and Cassie, so good to see you!" she greeted. "And this lovely girl must be Leigh." Eliza extended her hand to Leigh and continued, "Hank has told me you're new to North Side. I hope you are comfortable in your new home and happy with the school."

"Oh, yes, ma'am," Leigh replied.

"Well, I'm so pleased to hear that." Turning to Hank, Eliza offered: "Son, why don't you let your dad know you are here with your friends. He's down in the garage. Ask him if he'd like to come up and join you all for a little snack before we leave for the church building."

"Sure, Mom, will do." Hank responded. "You guys can go on into the den, and I'll be right back."

Eliza led the three into a comfortable den just off the kitchen, where a fireplace mantle laden with family pictures and framed awards held court. Leigh noticed above the mantle a large painting of what appeared to be Hank's mother at a young age, dressed in jeans and standing with her arm around the neck of a beautiful chestnut horse, with a mailbag hanging from the saddle. Turning to notice Leigh's gaze at the picture, Eliza said, "In case you're wondering about the painting, my dear husband had that done by a local artist from an old photograph. In my younger days, I carried the mail along the Trail of Tears—followed the river into Marion County and back."

"That must have been very exciting," Leigh commented, as she moved closer to the picture. "That's a beautiful horse."

"Oh, Sugar was just about everything to me, until Josh came along. We had some memorable times together. Thankfully, she lived out a peaceful old age with my family on the river after I gave up the mail route."

The sound of Nancy bouncing down the stairs and into the den was followed by her greeting: "Hey, Les! Hi, Cassie!" Extending her hand to Leigh, she said, "And you must be Leigh. Boy, your eyes are big and silvery even without the lenses! And the vitamins seem to be really helping—you're just right—and so are your feet!"

The girls laughed, as curiosity filled Les and he questioned, "What's the joke? Am I missing something?"

Cassie said, "Oh, I'll fill you in later. Let's just say Leigh is more than Nancy was expecting." She giggled as she turned to Leigh and said, "Who knew vitamins could work that fast!"

Hank and Josh came up the kitchen stairs and crossed into the den. Josh's rich, mellow voice greeted the group: "Les, good to see you again—and your pretty Cassie."

Cassie smiled, as Les responded, "Yes, sir, good to see you—and my girl is still as pretty and sweet as ever."

"I can certainly see that." Turning his attention to Leigh, Josh added politely, "And you are Miss Leigh Burkhart, I presume."

Leigh extended her hand to Josh, saying, "Yes, sir, Mr. Hodge. I'm pleased to meet Hank's dad."

"Well," Josh announced, "I'm glad you are spending a little time with us and will be with us this evening for worship. It's a fine way to end a beautiful day, and we have a nice group of young people you'll enjoy."

From the kitchen, Eliza entered carrying a tray with glasses of lemonade and a plate stacked with sandwiches. "How about some food to keep you going until you fill up on ice cream later."

"Super! Thanks, Mom," responded Hank, in chorus with the others' expressions of gratitude. "Mom makes a mean ham and cheese!" he proclaimed with a laugh, as he immediately reached for a sandwich.

"Hank, mind your manners," Eliza scolded, "wait for your guests."

"I need to taste-test them," Hank teased. "Besides, these aren't 'guests'—they're just Cassie, Les, and Leigh—like part of the family!"

Placing her glass on the hearth, Leigh settled in one of two armchairs in front of the fireplace and watched the interaction of the group before her. She felt warm and comfortable in the company of the Hodges, with Les and Cassie and, especially, with Hank. *This is what family should be*, she thought—not an uncomfortable tension when father enters the room, not an insecure anticipation of what might happen—disruption of peace, the back of an angry hand, another wound on a heart that had begun to grow calloused and insensate. No, in this room there was "the light…the spring of hope," about which Mr. Sanders had spoken—and she wanted to remain a part of it.

Chapter 20

The bell was ringing as Leigh placed her history book on the desk behind her. Likely the book was unnecessary—their fellow students seemed to respect her saving a seat for Hank, who was not only popular and well-liked for his athleticism and good-natured humor but respected for his character and the equity of his leadership.

Leigh decided she'd work on the Algebra II assignment first and placed the English Lit book on the shelf under her seat. As she did, her hand brushed against a folded piece of construction paper, and she was reminded of the letter Hank had mentioned. Retrieving the single cream-colored sheet, she unfolded it and read the words written in Hank's flourishing penmanship:

Dear Leigh,

These last few weeks have been the best, all because of you. You are the first girl I've dated, but I believe you will be the last girl I ever want to be part of my life. I hope someday you will feel the same about me.

In my thoughts and dreams, you are my future. If you think you might share these dreams, keep this note near to remind you of how I feel; but, if you

think me foolish, then destroy this note and tell me to wake up to reality.
    Hank

Leigh wiped tears with the hem of her sleeve before they could stream down her cheeks. There was a space of about three inches at the bottom of the note. She carefully folded the blank part up and pressed the crease with the side of her pencil. Then, she folded the paper the opposite way and creased it again, to make the fold line sharp before tearing the paper straight and neat across the page. In her most legible cursive, she wrote: *Please keep me in your dreams, and I will keep you in mine. Love, Leigh.* She turned to the history book on the desk behind her and slipped the note inside the front cover, so that a part was visible, on which she had drawn a small heart. She folded twice the remaining piece of paper with Hank's message and placed it in her bag. Then, she waited for Hank to arrive in study hall.

Leigh looked up from the text on which she was trying to focus and smiled at Hank as he entered the room and approached the seat. She waited for a moment before she felt a tap and reached behind her to retrieve the book that had reserved Hank's desk. She noticed her return note was missing, and then she felt Hank's hand on her shoulder. It lingered there

111

with a gentle squeeze—a silent confirmation of their relationship and of their mutual affection. Leigh shrugged her shoulder and leaned her head so that it rested briefly on Hank's hand. For the remainder of the study period, they sat in comfortable silence as they worked on their assignments. For the time, there was nothing more to say, and work completed now meant more uninterrupted time together later.

Chapter 21
November 1941

The days were now too cool for comfort outside the building, but Nancy found her library nook provided an enveloping warmth and peaceful solitude that opened her mind and sharpened her focus. The environment seemed to facilitate absorption of information and to stimulate the very process of analysis and application of what she was learning. She was growing in knowledge; but, beyond that, she could see how that knowledge would be incorporated into her profession, how it would be the foundation and the catalyst for further growth and development of her medical mind and skills.

Nancy leaned back in the desk chair, clenched her hands, and, yawning, stretched her arms above her head. She had finished the calculus assignment and smiled as she remembered the Wordsworth poem from childhood: "I shot an arrow into the air. It fell to earth I knew not where." *Well, let's see*, she thought with a giggle, *given the angle of the trajectory and the speed of the projectile ...*

"Is this a private joke, Miss Burkhart, or might you share it?"

Nancy looked up to see the smiling face of Jeffrey Langston standing on the other side of the study table. She laughed, "Oh, no, Mr. Langston. I was just thinking about calculus."

"How interesting. I don't remember calculus as a source of amusement during my study."

"Well, I would explain, but you'd think me a silly ninny," she replied.

"This quarter you've proven yourself far from being a ninny," he countered, "rather an exceptional student with an admirable work ethic."

"Why, thank you, Mr. Langston. I appreciate your saying that." Nancy noticed he pushed his glasses up on his nose and seemed to struggle with further communication. She continued, "I plan to attend medical school, and I need to develop and maintain good study habits now."

"Oh, a challenging and noble goal. Wise of you to recognize the importance of...um...good study habits," he stammered.

Nancy noticed Mr. Langston was becoming flushed and seemed uncomfortable, and she wondered at his sudden appearance and his lingering in her study area.

"Perhaps, Miss Burkhart," when this quarter is finished, "I could ask you to have lunch or dinner with me. I would like to talk with you about your future plans." Nancy's surprise must have been apparent, for he continued, haltingly, "I hope you are not offended by my suggestion. You might call it strictly a meeting of professional minds. As long as I am your lab instructor, it would not be proper for me to ask you for what some might consider a date, but even a date would not be improper when our class is finished."

"Why, Mr. Langston, thank you for the invitation," Nancy responded. "That would be very nice." She smiled at the obvious relief that washed over Jeffrey Langston's face, before he left a hasty, "Well, have a good day," in his wake and retreated around the bookshelves in Dewey's 500s section.

Nancy chuckled to herself. Jeffrey Langston was a handsome, intelligent, well-dressed gentleman. She wondered how he could be so uneasy around her. But, then again, she had grown up with the overt masculinity and strength of her father and even Hank, who now, thanks to Leigh, was progressing from his girl-shyness. Nancy felt—hoped, her nature was like her mother's, that she had acquired the independence and courage of her mother, Eliza McNeal. Whenever Nancy thought about her future, she saw herself in solitary pursuits, forging a way through higher education and a challenging profession without having the support or partnership of a husband. But even Eliza had found love and a life with Josh Hodge. Perhaps Nancy thought, her vision of her future should be more of a sketch than a finished picture. *Man proposes ... God disposes*, she thought.

She really didn't want to wrap herself in the same shell of academia in which Jeffrey Langston seemed to be encased—a shell purposefully constructed of intelligence and scientific pursuits. She wanted to feel at ease and comfortable, at the same time, professional and proficient in the world of medicine. Poor Mr. Langston—maybe he just needed some encouragement to break out of his shell, to escape from the laboratory. Nancy laughed as she thought of Jeffrey Langston smashing beakers and vials and Bunsen burners to get to the "Exit" door. She thought, *Well, we'll see what happens when finals are* over, then opened her lab manual to review the upcoming experiment.

Chapter 22
December 6, 1941

Rose Burkhart was sitting in the kitchen nook with her third cup of coffee, when Leigh entered to ask, "Mom, I just got off the phone with Hank. Do you mind if I go to worship with his family tomorrow?"

Rose stirred her coffee idly, as she pondered her response, then replied, "No dear, I don't have a problem with that. Will you be back in time for dinner with us?"

"Oh, yes, I should be back in time to help without keeping you waiting."

Charles Burkhart entered the kitchen and removed the pipe from his mouth to question, "And are you proposing to go to church with that boy again?"

"Yes, sir. It won't interfere with anything you have planned. The Hodges are good people. They said Alice and my parents are invited too, anytime."

"They're Bible-thumping Bible-belters!" he growled. "And you leave your sister out of this."

"No, sir," Leigh countered, "they are kind and loving. All of their friends have been nice to me."

"They're brainwashing you," he argued, as he took a cup from the cabinet. "Just don't be bringing any of that rubbish home with you."

"Charles, please…don't talk like that—that's just…just blasphemous," Rose pleaded.

"Don't be countering me," he warned Rose.

Leigh argued: "Why should you be concerned? What do you care? You'd rather we just be nothing than be religious—and that just might make you a better person."

With a burst of anger, Charles Burkhart threw the cup at Leigh, she dodged, and it smashed against the nook table. Rose shielded her face from the flying porcelain remnants, but a sharp piece grazed Leigh's cheek.

Leigh touched her face and then noted blood on her fingers. She glared at Charles. "I will be out of this house as soon I can. And, whenever I can, I will bring Mom and Alice to be with me. Maybe, when you are a lonely old man with no one to kick around and no one who loves you, you will realize what you have done to yourself and to your family." Leigh retreated to her room, leaving Rose in tears and leaving Charles Burkhart to mull over her threat and the future that lay before him.

Chapter 23
December 7, 1941, 9:00 A. M.

The Hodges' family car stopped in front of the Burkharts' walk, and Hank got out to make his way to the door. The day was clear and sunny, unlike some the last few weeks, when he had retrieved Leigh with an umbrella to protect her Sunday dress. Leigh seemed to enjoy the time she had shared with the Hodges. She told him her family was not at all religious, and she was eager to understand the faith that seemed to unite Hank's family with love and mutual respect.

The door opened and Leigh was on the porch before Hank made the last step and the first knock. "I was looking for you," she said.

"Good morning!" Hank said with a chipper grin. "I ordered this beautiful day just for a special girl."

Leigh replied, "Well, I'm sure she appreciates your thoughtfulness."

As they made their way down the steps to the walkway, Hank noticed the scratch on her face and quipped, "I see you cut yourself shaving this morning."

"Oh, that, well…no…long story," Leigh hesitated.

River Sisters, the Strangers

Hank perceived there was a thread of something troubling behind her words, and he planned to make time for her story as soon as they could be alone.

Chapter 24
December 7, 1941, 12:15 P. M.

"What a beautiful Sunday morning—maybe a bit chilly, but the sunshine is surely welcome," Eliza announced, as she came up the garage steps to the kitchen and laid her hat aside on the table. "I'll finish up dinner, just as soon as I take off these heels and get comfortable." Eliza made her way toward the master bedroom with the parting words, "Leigh surely looked pretty today, didn't she Hank?"

"She always does," replied Hank, who turned to Nancy adding, "Have to keep her supplied with those vitamins."

Nancy laughed and teased, "I hope she realizes by now why we call you Jug Head!"

As he passed through the kitchen, Hank walked by the covered cake plate and lifted the lid to swipe some icing with his finger."

"Hank, enough of that," warned his father. "You'll mess up your mother's cake."

"Yes, sir," he replied with a grin, "I hope to clean up a lot of the mess after dinner." Hank made his way up the stairs two steps at a time, as he untied his tie. "Dad, I'll help you get the car cleaned out and we can wash it after we eat, if you want to."

"Sounds good, son. I want it in good shape tomorrow if they expect me to take the guys visiting the dock to the train station."

Nancy followed Hank to her bedroom, calling behind, "Mom, I'll be right down after I change my dress." She heard her mother's muted response: "Thanks, dear."

Josh crossed the den and living room to the front door to collect the morning's paper, waiting there for him on the outside mat as usual. Seeing him glancing through its pages as she went into the kitchen, Eliza asked, "Any news?"

"No, nothing special. Roosevelt's still dancing around getting involved in conflict. And a lot of society hoopla, as usual." He continued with disappointment in his voice: "But, look at this. You want to tell me why Les Thompson didn't make the All-City Team? That's a real oversight."

"Well, Josh, I guess they can't put all the outstanding players on the team."

"No, but the same four teams are represented, it seems, year after year."

"Josh, go put some nice music on the radio and put your feet up and relax before dinner. We'll have it on the table in a jiffy."

He responded, "I'll just go change my clothes, so Hank and I can work on the car after we eat." He went toward the master bedroom shaking his head: "That All-Stars team makes absolutely no sense."

The smell of baked chicken wafted through the downstairs, as Eliza took the juicy, golden-brown bird from the oven. Nancy entered the kitchen and her mother directed, "Nancy, just set the table and pour the tea. I'll mash the potatoes." Then smiling, she whispered to her daughter: "We need to get some food into your father and Hank. He'll be disappointed too when he sees the All-Star list. Can't think of anything that might elevate their mood except food."

Nancy giggled as she took the glasses from the cabinet. "And that chocolate cake will give all of us a pick-me-up."

Chapter 25
December 7, 1941, 2:30 P. M.

Charles Burkhart lounged in his armchair in a delicious, aromatic cloud of wild honey and pecan pipe smoke. His feet, shod in his favorite fur-lined brown leather house slippers, rested on the ottoman. He was warm and comfortable in his favorite burgundy cardigan, with tan woven leather buttons fastened to hold his tie in alignment. Expelling his breath of frustration, he rested his head on the chair back, as he listened to the Bears and Cardinals championship game at Comiskey Park. He had pulled for the Bears all season from this position of comfort, wishing he were still there in the stands to add his voice to those cheering them on to NFL victory. Now, the Bears were behind fourteen points and...

A burst of static from the radio jolted his head upright, as he heard the announcer break into the broadcast: "We interrupt this game to announce that the Japanese have attacked the naval base at Pearl Harbor, Hawaii. We have no further information at this time. All military servicemen at today's game must report to your units immediately." Charles sat up and leaned forward, his hands clenched, elbows on his knees, as the announcer said: "I repeat: The

Japanese have attacked the naval base at Pearl Harbor, Hawaii. All military servicemen at today's game must report to your units immediately. We will return to the game in a few moments."

Charles turned the radio dial to pick up another station and caught the final words:

"...announces Japanese attacks on Pearl Harbor. This is Columbia Broadcasting calling Honolulu...go ahead Honolulu...This is Columbia Broadcasting in America calling Honolulu...go ahead Honolulu." The airwaves were suspended in silence.

There seemed to be a pulse throbbing in his head, in sync with the pounding of his heart. His younger brother, Roger, was in Honolulu—a machinist mate on the USS Arizona. They had been separated by time and distance and an age difference of some fourteen years, but he was the last remaining of Charles' immediate family. If there was any warmth in the memories of the home and family of his birth, they were attached to Roger, the "kid brother," not only under Charles' feet, but in Charles' heart. Never did he fail to send a card on Roger's birthday and on holidays—or call him, depending on where the Navy had stationed him. And every few months, Charles would pick up the phone and hear, "Hiya, big Charlie, how goes it?"

Roger had joined the Navy and left Chicago not long before Jack was killed...Jack, who was so much like Roger, not only in his boyish, blonde good looks, but in his exuberant, positive attitude toward life and living it to the fullest. Charles buried his face in his hands and tried to visualize Roger. The image kept changing, Roger into Jack, Jack into Roger. Jack, his one true friend, had helped ease the sense of loss Charles had felt when Roger was so far away— then, Jack got himself killed. In some way, Charles blamed Jack for his own death—always so intent on getting to the bottom of the crime that plagued his precinct, that crime usually coming from one well-connected, disreputable "family."

Charles knew he had sought Rose, who was his only link to Jack and, in some way, to Roger. He had gained Jack's wife and Jack's child, but they couldn't replace the warmth of life that was Jack and, by similarity and association in Charles' mind, the spirit that was Roger.

"Charles, are you all right?" Rose, having finished her chores in the kitchen and some sewing in the utility room, had come into the living room to take a seat near the radio.

Charles didn't respond for several seconds. Questions tumbled over each other in his mind: *Wouldn't I know, wouldn't I feel it if Roger was killed? What can I do—can I pray? That used to get me nothing—no relief from the cruelty that was my father, no escape from the milquetoast woman who*

126

was my mother. He remembered Rose's words—she said he was a blasphemer. *He probably wouldn't listen to me if I did pray.*

"Charles?" Rose asked again. When Charles looked up, Rose was stricken by the fearful vulnerability of his expression. "What has happened, Charles?"

"The Japanese have bombed the Navy base at Pearl Harbor," came his soft and measured response.

"Oh, no, Charles. Isn't that where Roger is stationed?"

"Yes. There are no other reports right now. We'll just have to wait for details. The news people can't even get a response back from Honolulu right now. This means we're at war."

Rose came to Charles and sat on the ottoman in front of him. "Charles, I am afraid—for Roger, for our family…"

Charles, head still in his hands, heard the words—and saw the face of his mother, the woman who cried and cringed without speaking or intervening when his father's heavy hand of "justice" came down upon his frail seven-year-old body.

Rose continued: "And I am so sorry—truly, that Roger may be involved." Charles was motionless, unseeing. "Charles, I need you, please, to be here for us. And I want you to know that I am here for you and want to help if there is something I can do—anything. Or you can push me away, if that's what you want, and I will leave you alone to deal with your worry, and I will handle my fear and everything else by myself. But so many times I have thought, if you can't love me, just be my friend."

Rose's words seemed to bring his thoughts into some kind of order: Roger, his grown-up kid brother—a man, perhaps now killed or injured doing the job he had chosen; Jack, a true friend, killed in the line of duty doing a job he loved; parents now dead—abusive father, enabling mother. Who was left? This woman, a wife who should have engendered devotion because of his friend and affection because of her own sweet, gentle nature.

Time seemed interminable while Rose waited for Charles' response. Finally, she sighed and moved to stand from the ottoman. With a suddenness that startled her, Charles reached out to take her arm and pulled her back to the seat—not with anger or force, but with the hand of one in need of support and with eyes, it seemed, pleading for companionship and understanding.

Jan Dearman

Chapter 26
December 7, 1941, 8:00 P. M.

Josh Hodge answered the knock at the front door and opened it to find Les Thompson, cap in hand, pacing as he awaited a response. "Les, come in. I assume you've heard about the attack."

"Yes, sir, that's why I'm here. I wanted to talk to Hank."

"Sure, come along. He's back in the den. We were just listening to the reports coming in, though there's not much detail yet. What we do hear doesn't sound good."

"No, sir. The Japanese have been hard at it, even while their envoys were here talking peace."

"This morning Hank and I were upset about your not making the All-Stars. I guess all this war talk has put that in perspective." Josh added, "We hadn't turned the radio on this afternoon, so we didn't even hear about the attack till we got to the building for worship this evening. We had a prayer service, and I don't think any people prayed harder or louder than we prayed this evening." Josh went to the window looking out over the back yard and stood, hands in pockets, to listen to the disturbing news.

"Hey, Les." Hank motioned for Les to take a seat near the radio. "There's a report just now coming through from some reporter up on the roof of a building in Honolulu." Hank checked the accuracy of the tuner and increased the volume, as a reporter read: "I am speaking to you from Honolulu, where for three hours a fierce attack, undoubtedly by the Japanese, has been going on against the United States military base at Pearl Harbor. The city of Honolulu also has been heavily damaged. I have a view of the severe bombing from my vantage point. However, I have no details on the extent of the destruction or the specific targets that have been hit. All residents of Honolulu have been advised to seek shelter in their homes or in places of safety away from the military installations. We will update as we can. This is real—we are at war on the land and on the sea." The station returned to the music of the Philharmonic.

The deceptive tranquility of the music was broken by Les: "Hank, I'm enlisting in the Army tomorrow. They're going to need all the men they can get. I want to serve, and I figure they'll be lowering the draft age before long. I want to go to them before they come for me."

Josh turned to hear Hank's response: "Yeah, Les, I understand. But I won't even be seventeen till March."

Josh could feel the increasing pressure in his chest and the breathlessness that had afflicted him so many weeks ago. He reached for the case in his pocket and turned back toward the window to avoid detection while placing a small pill under his tongue. He tried to maintain his composure as he moved toward the fireplace to sit in one of the armchairs.

Les responded, "I know. I just wanted you to know what I intend to do. I don't know what that means for me about graduation. Maybe they'll delay me until June. Or maybe I can finish half a year early, though I don't have the grades or credits your sister had."

"Well, I have the grades and the credits—maybe Mr. McConnell will recommend me for an early out," Hank replied.

"Son." Josh's breath was shallow. "Please just wait this out. You should graduate with your class, then make that kind of decision."

"Dad, I'll be seventeen in three months. I don't know where this war will be then, but I want to be ready. This country is going to need every man fit to serve."

His mind raced with his pulse, as Josh contemplated the boy, his son, who was transforming before his eyes into a man with purpose and determination. "Son, I can't lose you, like Morgan lost Caleb."

"Dad, Uncle Morgan and Aunt Maddie grieved, but Caleb was a decorated hero, and they have hope of seeing him again when this life is over. We talk about having faith, but the time comes when we have to prove it."

Josh wanted to shout and demand obedience, but how could he argue with Hank? How could he deny the courage and conviction of the two he saw before him? He had wanted to forge his son into a man of maturity and responsibility—a man of strength, spiritual character, leadership. Now, a potentially devastating war had realized that goal—far too soon. "But, son, you're not even seventeen," Josh repeated, pleading.

Eliza entered the room and caught Josh's last few plaintive words. Nodding a greeting to Les, she asked, "What's going on, Josh?" Nancy followed behind Eliza but stopped at the entrance, not wanting to enter the cloud of anxiety that seemed to pervade the den.

"Mom, Les is going to enlist, and I want to enlist with him," stated Hank. "I know I won't be seventeen until March. They may not take me for months, even years, but I want to make the commitment."

Eliza dropped into the armchair facing Josh. She weighed her words before speaking: "And Josh, what do you say?"

With resignation, Josh said again, "Eliza, he's not even seventeen. He should graduate first and then see where we are in this war."

Hank interrupted, "Mom, what if I can finish early, like Nancy—what then? Would you give me permission to serve?"

Eliza remembered herself at sixteen—and the determination to prove herself strong and capable, riding horseback on the Trail with saddlebags sometimes half her weight. When she thought about her mother's concern and her own fearlessness at that age, she understood her son, but also her husband—and her own longing to turn back time. Where was the baby she had nursed, the toddler she had shielded from his sister's overly energetic love, the teenager she only recently had advised about girls and dating? She noticed Les, who seemed uncomfortable in the midst of their family discussion. She appreciated his quiet reserve and retreat from interference.

Eliza spoke in words measured in understanding of both her husband and her son. "Hank, I understand, and I am proud of you and Les for your conviction and patriotism. But also, I understand your father's concern, and I share his concern. Morgan and Madeline have been where your father and I are, and they endured the worst possible outcome of Caleb's decision. They grieved mightily at his death. Granted, likely, they are stronger people for the faith that sustained them—and continues to sustain them. This decision is one for you to make, but only with your father's blessing. Of course, whenever you come of age, any decision and its consequences are your responsibility."

Josh listened to his wife's words and remembered the vibrance and daring of the young Eliza. At Hank's age, she had plunged headlong into her chosen work, willing to accept the difficulties, even the perils that might come with it. How could he deny Hank this challenge any more than he had been able to deny Eliza, when she was determined to ride the Trail even after they married?

All waited for Josh's response. When he spoke, he said, "If you can graduate early, like your sister, I will support your decision—when you are of age to be accepted for enlistment."

"Thanks, Dad" was Hank's simple reply.

"Les," Josh continued, "what have your parents said about your decision?"

"Well, sir," Les answered, "they hope I will have two or three more years before I actually have to deploy. But we all know that depends on what happens in the next several days. Mom and Dad are just like you, sir, worried, but supportive."

"Yes, well," admitted Josh, "really what more can we do? The future is yours, and you must work, even fight, to make it what you want it to be—

for yourselves and your children someday." Josh wiped tears welling in his eyes. "It just seems the whole world will be fighting against you."

Hank moved to hug his father and whispered, "I love you, Dad."

"I love you, too, son—and I'm really very proud of you—proud of both you young men."

Chapter 27
December 8, 1941

Coach Leonard's study hall was abuzz with quiet conversations. Before Monday morning's tardy bell, those who had not heard the radio news broadcast, interrupting the Sunday game, endured the shock and horror of those who had listened the previous afternoon. Throughout the day, teachers had allowed students liberty to converse, assuming they might find in each other some comfort and sense of stability. The security of mundane teenage lives had been lost in the unpredictable future of a suddenly upheaved adult world.

The telling and retelling of the events took precedence in every hour, regardless of the subject—except, of course, in history class. There, Mr. Sanders had spoken thoughtful, measured words: "The recent activity of humanity has left a dramatic and indelible imprint on the record of time. Only God in heaven knows—and time will tell, what lies in store for nations on both sides of the oceans to our East and to our West." The gravity of his statement quieted the class, as every student absorbed his explanation of the geopolitical situation that culminated in the attack on Pearl Harbor.

Study hall was usually their time to pass notes, and Leigh loved Hank's surprisingly romantic nature. Only last Friday, he had slipped a note over Leigh's shoulder that professed, "You are my first love and the only girl for me. I'll wait for you the rest of my life." Today, there was no note, and Hank was unusually quiet.

Leigh turned around in her desk seat toward him. He was frowning as he scribbled in his notebook. Leigh's voice tremored as she whispered, "Do you think we'll be attacked?"

"What do you mean, Leigh? We have been attacked! Hawaii is our territory and Pearl Harbor our naval base!"

Obviously, he was frustrated with her. He had seemed distant or distracted during the day, and now he was upset. "I'm sorry, Hank. I meant here on the mainland. I didn't mean to make you mad. I'm just afraid of what might happen."

Hank softened as he looked up at Leigh. "I'm sorry. I've had a lot on my mind." He studied her gray eyes, glistening with tears, and added, "We don't know what the future's going to be for any of us now, Leigh."

Coach Leonard's voice interrupted, as he announced: "I have just received word from the principal's office that an assembly has been called in the auditorium. You have five minutes to go to your lockers; then, go directly there. Don't congregate in the halls."

Hank closed his notebook and stood, reaching out for her hand. "Come on, Leigh. If you get there before I do, wait for me outside the auditorium, so we can sit together."

As she made her way through the hall traffic, Leigh saw Cassie coming out of Mrs. Swain's English class. "Hey, Cass, wait up!"

Cassie slowed her pace to wait for her friend. "I don't have much time. I'm meeting Les at his locker after I pick up my books and sweater."

"I'm meeting Hank outside the auditorium after I get my things. Maybe we can all sit together."

"I'll tell Les. We'll wait for you. But hurry so we can get four seats together."

Hank seemed anxious, chewing on his thumb, as Leigh scurried toward the assembly. "Hey, there," she called. "Les and Cassie are meeting us, so we can sit together."

"They just went in to get us seats. Come on," he urged, taking her arm and guiding her through the door.

Les was standing about half-way down the center aisle, as they made their way around students holding seats or moving into their path to allow others entrance to a row.

"We got four together, including the aisle seat," Les stated, as they moved into their places. Hank led the way past Les into the row, so the two girls would sit between them. "I did have to throw around a little senior weight to get those guys to move over for us," he grinned, gesturing toward Al Griffin and Seth Harvey, seated beyond Hank.

The microphone squealed briefly, gaining the students' attention, before the principal's voice, jarring and stern, projected over the audience: "Students, please take your places as quickly as possible. Be seated and remain quiet, as we have an urgent and important announcement. It pertains to yesterday's attack on the United States Naval Base at Pearl Harbor, Hawaii."

Movement and sound drained from the interior of the auditorium, as a wave of silence and anxious anticipation flowed over the student body.

Mr. McConnell continued: "At 12:30 P.M. today, President Franklin Roosevelt spoke to a Joint Session of the United States Congress. The address was carried by radio, and our secretary, Miss Nance, took the dictation as he spoke. I would like to read the transcription she has prepared:

River Sisters, the Strangers

"Yesterday, December 7, 1941—a date which will live in infamy—the United States of America was suddenly and deliberately attacked by naval and air forces of the Empire of Japan. The United States was at peace with that nation and, at the solicitation of Japan, was still in conversation with its government and its emperor looking toward the maintenance of peace in the Pacific. Indeed, one hour after Japanese air squadrons had commenced bombing in the American island of Oahu, the Japanese ambassador to the United States and his colleague delivered to our Secretary of State a formal reply to a recent American message. And while this reply stated that it seemed useless to continue the existing diplomatic negotiations, it contained no threat or hint of war or of armed attack. It will be recorded that the distance of Hawaii from Japan makes it obvious that the attack was deliberately planned ..."

Leigh noticed as Les leaned over and whispered to Cassie, and Cassie replied, "No, Les, please!" Cassie grabbed his arm, and Les placed his hand over hers and continued speaking in words only Cassie could hear.

"...many American lives have been lost. In addition, American ships have been reported torpedoed on the high seas between San Francisco and

Honolulu. Yesterday the Japanese government also launched an attack against Malaya.

"Last night Japanese forces attacked Hong Kong. Last night Japanese forces attacked ..."

Les leaned forward and waved his hand to catch Hank's attention and gave him a thumbs-up. Hank nodded in return. He picked up his books and jacket from the floor in front of him.

Leigh grasped his arm and whispered, "Hank, what's going on? What's wrong?" The urgency in Leigh's voice, the fear on her face, betrayed the panic squeezing her chest. "Please, tell me." The principal's voice faded from her hearing:

"...The people of the United States have already formed their opinions and well understand the implications to the very life and safety of our Nation.

"As Commander in Chief of the Army and Navy I have directed that all measures be taken for our defense. But always will our whole Nation remember the character of the onslaught..."

Hank leaned close, putting his hands over hers. "Leigh, no matter what happens, remember, I want a future with you. But we must make sure we have a future. Les and I are enlisting. I love you, Leigh." He kissed her cheek, then looked at Les, who was waiting on Hank's next move, and said, "Let's go."

They both stood as Mr. McConnell's words powered an unseen force moving through the assembly:

"No matter how long it may take us to overcome this premeditated invasion, the American people in their righteous might will win through to absolute victory. I believe…"

Les stepped out into the aisle, as Hank moved past Cassie and Leigh, now holding hands as tears lined their cheeks.

Mack Frasier, sitting down front, stood; then, Fred Gentry, next to him. They moved toward the rear exit. Then, Sonny Harrison, across the way; then, the Compton boy from Algebra II.

Mr. McConnell paused, as he noticed the young men leaving the assembly. A sob choked his words, before he composed himself to continue:

"I believe that I interpret the will of the Congress and of the people when I assert that we will not only defend ourselves to the uttermost but will make it very certain that this form of treachery shall never again endanger us."

Heads followed the movements, as one or two boys here, there, from the front, in the back, once a group of three, stood and moved to the auditorium exit. At times, muffled sobs or whispered pleas, "No, don't go!" interrupted the quiet background of Mr.

McConnell's reading. From moment to moment, he watched them leave without remonstration:

"...with the unbounding determination of our people—we will gain the inevitable triumph—so help us God."

After a moment to regain his failing composure, Mr. McConnell came to the end of his reading:

"I ask that the Congress declare that since the unprovoked and dastardly attack by Japan on Sunday, December 7, 1941, a state of war has existed between the United States and the Japanese Empire."

The principal's gaze encompassed the auditorium, now with several empty seats. He watched the double doors close behind the Jessop twins—fraternal in their appearance, but like one mind shared between two individuals in their similar personalities and interests. He continued: "It is my sad duty to inform you that little more than an hour after President Roosevelt's speech, the Congress declared war on Japan." Taking the handkerchief from his pocket, he wiped his eyes, and continued: "Students, let's all bow our heads and engage in a moment of silent prayer for our nation and for your brave fellow students—volunteers, who have left our ranks, determined to protect our freedom and our way of life."

A full minute passed before Mr. McConnell's quavering voice sounded through the assembly. "May God have mercy on our nation and on the precious souls of those who seek to defend her. May God bless our young men and the young women who serve and support their efforts." He again surveyed the audience, then, stated: "You may be dismissed to go to your homes."

Cassie and Leigh, like many others, remained in their seats. Some girls shared tears or consoling embraces; some, only words of disbelief. Some of the older boys seemed troubled, conflicted: *Should they stay or leave with the others?* Many of the younger boys were angry: *If only they were just a year or two older!*

Millie and Alice were among the first girls to rise from their seats to look around the assembly in search of their sister and cousin.

"There they are!" Alice took Millie's arm and pulled her toward Leigh and Cassie. She took the seat Les had vacated and asked, "What's going on? I don't understand. How could they just get up and leave and Mr. McConnell not say a word?"

"Because we're at war," Cassie told Alice, "They're enlisting to fight. Les said, 'It's time to grow up and be men. We're not schoolboys, not anymore.'"

Leigh felt literally shaken and her body ached. Unabashedly, she allowed the silent tears to stream over her cheeks, and the only words that resounded through her thoughts were those of Mr. Sanders: *These are the worst of times...the winter of despair.*

Chapter 28
March 1942

Charles Burkhart parked the car in the driveway and plodded up the back steps to the kitchen door. Since Pearl Harbor, he had felt no impulse to assuage his anxiety in the night life of the golf club or on the links, regardless of the luxuriance of the greens, fairways, and manicured grounds surrounding them. His solace had been Rose's quiet, calm, steady nature—and, perhaps, some faint hope that Roger might still be alive or recuperating in a hospital somewhere. There had been no word, but Roger might not have updated the family's address in his personnel file since Charles had moved his family to the South.

Only in the months since the bombing had Charles begun to realize that Rose could be his wife and companion, no longer belonging to Jack. Their relationship could be one without ghosts of the dead, friend or family. The guilt and fear that had motivated his often cruel and unkind actions were dissolving in understanding of their source: loss and loneliness, wanting what Jack had, and then, assuming what Jack had could never really be his. He had lashed out in fear, anger, and frustration—becoming what his father was and cloaking Rose in the persona

Jan Dearman

of his mother. Jack had been his friend, and he had
failed to be what Jack would have wanted for Rose
and Leigh. But, perhaps, all that could change.

Rose was sitting in the kitchen nook facing
the door when he entered. She needed no words to
tell him there was unwelcome news in the telegram
that lay in front of her on the table. Charles dropped
to the seat across from Rose. She pushed the envelope toward him. He pushed it back to her. "No,
Rose, please, you read it to me."

Rose ran her finger under the flap and removed the note inside. Just glancing at the first
words, tears began to pool in her eyes. "Charles, are
you sure you want me to read it?"

"Please, Rose."

"The Navy Department deeply regrets to inform you…" Rose stopped at the sound of Charles'
sob and waited for him to take out his pocket handkerchief.

"Go on," he directed.

"…that your brother Roger Raulston Burkhart,
Machinists Mate First Class USN was killed in action
in the performance of his duty and in the service of
his country, on December 7, 1941, at Pearl Harbor,
Oahu, Hawaii. The department extends to you its sin-
cerest sympathy in your great loss and apology for
the delay in this notification, our records having in-
correct information concerning next of kin. On account

147

of existing conditions, the body cannot be recovered. It is entombed with the bodies of hundreds of his naval comrades, who now serve as a symbol of service and patriotism that will rally the forces of our great nation against foreign aggression. Please do not divulge the name of his ship or station to prevent possible aid to our enemies." Rose added, "It is signed by the Rear Admiral, Chief of Naval Personnel."

Charles now was openly sobbing and wiping his eyes, and Rose came to stand next to him, drawing his weeping face into the fullness of her apron. "Charles, I am so sorry," she said, smoothing his hair as she comforted him. Charles wrapped his arms around her, clinging to her as if he might be sucked away by the storm of grief whirling around and through him.

At last Charles regained some composure and directed Rose: "Please, sit down, Rose."

Rose repositioned herself across from him and waited for him to speak. Charles dried his face and took a deep, halting breath. "Rose, I felt Roger's loss before it was ever confirmed by that telegram. He was all I had, or so I thought." Charles reached for Rose's hands. "I have been unfair to you and Leigh, and even to Alice. I know you married me out of fear and need, and I have resented you for not loving me as you loved Jack. Rather than be Jack's friend and, thereby, your friend, I became jealous of a dead man. I made myself miserable and bitter and lonely, and I blamed that misery on you. I have been so selfish. I am still trying to sort out things in my head to get some understanding of the man I have been—the man I am, but I want to try to be better, if you will be patient and help me."

"Charles, I promised to be your wife and your helper in every way. Honestly, I have felt more like your housemaid. But rather than deal with things openly, I have retreated with my thoughts and memories of Jack, thinking love could only be there. But Jack is gone. If we both accept that, store memories in the past—or erase them, and determine to build love and trust, we might be a real family."

"Thank you, Rose. I want that. I will try. I may fail at times, but I promise to try again and again."

Charles and Rose, holding hands, were facing each other across the kitchen table when Leigh and Alice returned from school and the front door closed behind them. Neither moved when the girls entered the room, when they saw their daughters' questioning surprise to see Rose and Charles in this unexpected position.

Rose said, "Charles, we start now, with honesty and acceptance of responsibility, all right?" He nodded in agreement. She directed: "Girls, please go sit at the dining room table. Charles and I want to talk to you."

When the girls joined Charles and Rose at the table, Charles began: "First, Leigh, let me ask your forgiveness for the anger I have shown. I have been so unkind—even hurting you at times. Can you forgive me?"

Leigh was at a loss for words. *Who was this man? What had happened to bring him to these knees of repentance?* So many questions swirled in her head, but she remembered words she had heard recently about forgiveness. She must forgive or she would not be forgiven. She could only shake her head in bewilderment and shrug: "I can try."

Alice put her hand over Leigh's, as Rose began to explain: "Today we received confirmation of your Uncle Roger's death at Pearl Harbor. Of course, Charles has been terribly upset about losing his brother." Rose continued carefully: "Losing the last member of his birth family has made him realize the importance of the family he has now. He doesn't have to feel alone. He has us. He wants to be a good father. We want to be good parents. We want a close, loving family. We have waited far too long to work to make that happen."

Leigh and Alice waited without speaking to see where this uncharted path would lead.

Charles interjected: "I have been a failure as a husband and father."

Rose took Charles' hand. "But I have not been a good wife or mother," she hesitated, "because I've been dishonest with both you girls. It was easier not to tell the truth, but more difficult for all of us to live with lies. I was afraid of what you'd think of me."

"But, Mom," Alice countered, "You're a wonderful mother."

"I want to be," replied Rose. She looked at Charles to hear, "It's time." She pulled two pictures from her apron pocket and placed the first in front of the girls. "Girls, this was Jack Stanfield, Charles' best friend. He was a police detective, killed in the line of duty. He was a wonderful man, and Charles and I loved him very much." Rose watched Leigh's expression, as she proceeded with care, placing the picture of herself with her father over the first of Jack by himself: "Jack was my first husband and your father, Leigh." Alice gasped and looked to Leigh for a reaction. Rose waited for Leigh to absorb the information.

Unable to tell if Leigh was hearing his words, Charles explained: "Leigh, your father was my true friend, and I wanted to take his place to help you and your mother. But I am not the man your father was. I could not take his place. Rather than make my own place, trying to be the best husband and father I could be, I became a bitter, jealous man who couldn't find happiness with a fine wife and beautiful daughter."

Her mother interjected: "And, Leigh, I was frightened and unable to support us by myself. Charles became our benefactor and then my husband. You were just a baby—I couldn't explain, then I didn't know how to explain, and finally I just didn't try."

A few seconds passed, then Leigh's dam of emotions burst: "You should have tried!" Leigh grabbed the pictures and sprang to her feet, knocking over the chair on which she had been seated. She shouted through her tears: "Why all the secrecy? Why did you let me live this lie all these years, thinking my own father hated me so much he'd rather give me the back of his hand than love me?"

Charles bowed his head as if beaten. Rose stood and tried to take Leigh in her arms: "Oh, dear, I am so sorry. I was afraid of what you'd think of me—weak and dependent and marrying within just months of your father's death. I was alone and afraid, and Charles was kind. But I still loved your father and didn't even try to love Charles as I should have."

"Leigh, we want to change all that," Charles pleaded. "We have to begin with honesty. We must try to build your trust. I want to change. I want to be the husband your mother needs and the father you girls deserve. I will try. I just ask you to give me a chance."

Leigh pulled away from her mother and ran from the room. Her feet sounded on the stairs before the door slammed on the bedroom she shared with Alice.

Rose sat down at the table and Charles put his arm around her shoulder. "She needs time to digest all this. She's lived in our lie for nearly seventeen years."

Alice remained seated and rested her forehead on her folded arms. When she spoke, she raised her head, eyes red from crying, and asked, "So Leigh and I are only half-sisters?"

"Yes, Alice," said Rose.

"Do you love her?" she asked her father.

Charles halted for a moment, then answered: "Yes, Alice, I love her. I haven't loved her as a father should love his child—and I certainly haven't shown her love, because in my confused mind, she belonged to Jack and couldn't be mine. But since she was a baby, she has been my daughter, my responsibility. In some way, I feel Jack entrusted her to me, and I have let him down."

"What happens now?" Alice asked.

Rose looked at Charles for confirmation and answered, "Your father and I are going to work on being each other's best friend. We hope you and Leigh will soon be able to accept there will be no more lies, no more secrets. We want to be a family who can share good times and bad times, with love and without fear."

Alice stood. "I'm going to check on Leigh." She started toward the hallway, then turned and asked, "If you're planning dinner, Leigh may not want to come back downstairs."

Charles said, "It has been a difficult afternoon for all of us. If you can persuade Leigh to join us, I'll take you girls and your mother out to dinner. Maybe six o'clock?"

I'll see." Alice seemed to contemplate each step as she went upstairs.

Chapter 29

Leigh was lying across her bed when Alice entered their room. Alice sat on the twin bed opposite her sister. She noticed Leigh still held the photos in her hand. "You want to talk?" she asked. She was silent and waited for Leigh's response.

"No," came the muffled reply.

"Well, okay, I'm here if you decide you want to." Alice tried to understand her own feeling of guilt. Hers was the same mother and father she had always known, but Leigh had just learned the father she had never known was the key to understanding everything in Leigh's life. This was something Alice could neither share nor understand. Alice had lived with truth, not lies about her parents. For the first time, there was a real wall between herself and her sister—not just the trivial differences of age and personality, but the real difference of their very being. Alice said, "I love you, Leigh, just like I always have. And I'll try to be a better sister. I know I'm an aggravation at times. But I'll never love you half—I'll always love you whole."

Leigh raised herself to sit cross-legged on the comforter. She wiped her eyes with the back of her hand and said, "You don't have to change. None of this is your fault."

"But I feel so bad. I feel like I've done something wrong."

Leigh noticed Alice's puffy red eyes. "No, Alice, this is all about our parents. We are hurting because of their decisions."

Alice brushed wet hair out of her face. "I feel bad because Dad was mean to you sometimes. Sometimes he just ignored me, but he never hurt me."

Leigh declared: "I told him I'd try to forgive him. Right now, I think I'm angrier with Mother for lying to me all these years."

"I don't understand it all—or why she felt the way she did, but you know Mom loves us." Alice waited for Leigh's response, then asked: "What are you going to do?"

"What can I do? I'm going to get out of this house as soon as I can make it on my own, but that won't be till I graduate."

"What are you going to do about Mom and Dad? How do you feel about them?" Alice continued.

"Right now, I still hate Dad for his meanness, and I realize Mom has lied to me. How would you feel?"

Alice thought, then spoke: "I don't know how I'd feel. I'm not you. I guess I'm scared that everything's changed all of a sudden. Things weren't great, but we sort of knew what to expect. Now, we don't know what will happen—what kind of parents we'll have from here on."

Leigh sighed. "I just don't know if I really can forgive Dad—*Charles*. And, if Mom was concerned about what I'd think of her, well, right now, it's not good. I'd understand about the marriage, maybe even her not telling me, but she was too weak to defend her own child when Dad would get so angry." Leigh looked at the picture of Jack Stanfield and sighed, "I wish he had lived. I wish I could have known my real father."

Alice tried to find wise words for her sister: "If your real father and Dad were such good friends, your real father must have seen the good in Dad and liked him as a person. Dad told me he loves you but has failed to show you. Do you think you can give him a chance—see if he can change?"

"I don't know." Leigh shook her head and sighed, "I just don't know."

Alice declared: "Leigh, I don't want to be mean, but your real father is dead. My real dad is alive and has asked you to forgive him and to give him a chance to be a good father. And Mom has said she's sorry for not telling you before now. The way I see it, they can't do any more. They've made some bad mistakes. They've asked for forgiveness and a chance to change. What more can they do? Seems to me, it's all up to us now—assuming, of course, they mean what they say and really try."

"Some family we are," Leigh declared.

"Yeah, but if they mean what they say about being better parents, nothing can change if we don't cooperate."

Alice and Leigh, both out of words to express the emotions they felt, sat in silence. Alice watched Leigh, who turned over the photo of Jack Stanfield,

River Sisters, the Strangers

to read on the back: *Jack, beloved husband, married June 10, 1922.* On the back of the other photo, also in her mother's distinctive handwriting, was the note: *Dad, soon to be Grandpa, and mother-to-be, Thanksgiving, 1923.*

Leigh, frowning and pensive, reached for the notepad and pencil on the bedside table and appeared to begin writing and calculating numbers.

"What are you doing?" Alice asked.

"Just a minute," she replied. "Alice, mother was born in November,1904, wasn't she?"

"Yeah, November 18, 1904."

"Well, the way I figure it, Mother was only seventeen when she married my father. They married in June before she turned eighteen."

"Wow, that was kind of young! That means they had only been married a little over a year when he was killed and then you were born in November of 1923."

"Yeah, Mom was still just maybe a year older than I am now. That seems really strange."

Alice thought for a moment and said, "Jack and Dad probably weren't a lot older than Mom." She proceeded, "Leigh, you just said you'll get out of the house as soon as you can make it on your own. Mom said she was alone with you and was scared and couldn't make it on her own. So, she turned to the man closest to Jack Stanfield, his best friend— and likely he was only in his twenties."

"So, what are you saying, Alice?"

158

"Well…I guess I'm saying we need to try to understand the way they might have been back then—not knowing much more than we do—and maybe give them a chance. Our fathers once loved and trusted each other. Our mother was alone and scared, and my father wanted to help you and the friend he loved. Somehow all their crazy emotions and ideas just messed everything up."

Leigh paused, then relented: "I guess I can try. Things won't get better unless I do. Mother showed more backbone this evening than I've ever seen, and Dad seemed really beaten down."

"Before I came up, he told me it has been a difficult day for all of us. He said he'd take us out to dinner if you want to go—about six o'clock."

"I don't really feel like eating anything. But I guess we've got to start sometime, don't we?"

Alice came to give her sister a hug. "I love you, Leigh—whole, not half, like I said. Let's try to help us be a family before you fly the coop next year."

Charles Burkhart was no stranger to the restaurant into which he escorted his family that evening. The hostess said, "Welcome, Mr. Burkhart. Table for four?"

"Yes, Karen, thank you. Karen, this is my wife, Rose. And these are my daughters, Leigh and Alice."

"I'm pleased to meet you, Mrs. Burkhart, and such lovely daughters." She led them to a round table near a window overlooking the course. Handing them each a menu, she added, "I hope you enjoy your meal."

No one had spoken during the ride to the country club. Charles broke the silence to say, "I don't know how hungry you are, but, please, order whatever you'd like. The food here is excellent. You won't be disappointed." He seemed to choke and lowered his gaze to the menu, as he added, "You've had enough disappointment for one day."

Rose laid her hand on Charles' arm. "Charles, we've had a rough start, but a start nonetheless."

Charles placed his hand over hers and responded, "Yes, Rose, a new day, I hope."

Alice looked at Leigh with an expression imploring her to speak.

Leigh said, "Dad, I told you I'll forgive you, and I will try to forget. I am going to try to forgive Mother's not telling me about my father. It seems he loved you both, and you both loved him. But he is gone, and we are here. I am willing to try to be the family he surely would have wanted us to be."

Charles said, "Leigh, thank you. Your father was a good man and a true friend. My befuddled mind has led me so far astray from what he would have wanted. It's a shame it took a terrible tragedy to realize the odious creature I had become."

"If my father loved you as his best friend, surely, I could learn to be your friend...and your daughter," Leigh allowed. Words came to her mind: light and darkness, hope and despair, everything and nothing, heaven and hell. Could there be one without the other? Not for long, it seemed, at least not in this day.

Chapter 30

Nancy had been so full of thoughts and emotions, she now felt empty, as if everything had spilled out and was gone. She forged down the long central hallway of the administration building, her feet determinedly marching toward Dr. Lawson's office. She prayed he would be available to see her. The decision was made, and she wanted the plan to be set and operational.

The door opened to face the desk of Dr. Lawson's secretary, who ended a call, returned the phone to its cradle, and asked, "Good morning, may I help you?"

"I'm Nancy Hodge, and I'd like to see Dr. Lawson, if he has a few free minutes."

"Well, I can check. You say your name is 'Nancy Hodge'?"

"Yes, ma'am." Nancy noticed the marble name plate stand on the front of the desk and added, "Miss Gains."

"Just a moment, Miss Hodge. Let me pull your file, and I will check with Dr. Lawson. Just have a seat."

"Thank you," replied Nancy, and she sat in the chair stationed by the door. It was upholstered in a blue floral tapestry fabric and had cushioned pads on the arms. With nervous anticipation, Nancy's heels tapped silently on the carpet, as she waited for Miss Gains to knock on Dr. Lawson's door and then, to gain access when a masculine voice declared, "Come in." Miss Gains entered and closed the door behind her. Nancy could hear only muffled communication.

She noted the morning's time, 8:50, on the large regulator clock hanging on the rich, dark, wood paneled wall to the right of the dean's door. Its pendulum seemed out of synchrony with the seconds that passed before Miss Gains returned and said, "Dr. Lawson is free to see you now."

Nancy said, "Thank you" and stood to proceed toward the open office door.

A deep, growly voice, affected by age and years of pipe smoke, greeted her: "Miss Hodge, how are you?" Dr. Lawson stood to shake her hand and motioned to the chair before him. "Please tell me what I can do for you. But first, let me tell you how pleased we are to have you at this university. You are proving yourself to be quite a diligent student. Your grades this quarter are outstanding. We are pleased we made the decision on your early entrance."

Nancy felt her cheeks warm at his unexpected praise. "Thank you, sir. I enjoy studying and learning. The experience has been very pleasant—very satisfying."

"Well, good, good," he responded. "I was fearful you might have some complaint with your time here."

"Oh, no, sir," Nancy assured him. Nancy took a deep breath and continued: "But, sir, I have decided to make a change in my course of study."

"Really? I thought you were determined to pursue a course leading to medical school."

"Well, sir, the recent developments—Pearl Harbor, the Declaration of War—times have changed, and I must change with them. Medical school is still in my future—obviously, I'm still young—but I want to enter the nursing program. I have several required courses under my belt, and by the time I complete training, I'll be twenty-one. As soon as I am licensed, I can enlist to serve as a nurse. When the war is over, then I can go to medical school. I'll still be in my twenties."

Nancy waited for his response. Dr. Lawson studied the file that lay open in front of him—far too long, it seemed, for him to grasp the information contained in its sparse contents.

He inhaled, cleared his throat, pushed his glasses up the bridge of his nose, and asked, "Are you very sure about this? Have you spoken to your parents? Do you understand the gravity of this decision?"

Nancy sensed genuine, personal concern in his voice, and she noted the deepening creases at the corners of his eyes. But she recognized this as the time to verbalize the words formed and practiced in her head—for days, they had swirled like leaves, but now were calm and settled on firm ground. "Yes, sir, I am very sure. I have not spoken to my parents yet. They will not be pleased, but they will respect my decision. I do understand this course may entail some future risk, but I must pursue it. My brother has enlisted with my parents' permission and expects to be called up whenever the Army will accept him. His best friend is in training as we speak. I want to prepare to be there—perhaps not for them, but for others like them, who need the best care I can give." Nancy waited.

Again, Dr. Lawson cleared his throat. "Miss Hodge, I admire and respect your decision." He took a form from a drawer of files in the credenza behind him. Making a few notes on the paper and signing the bottom with the flourish of his signature, he added: "I will help you make this change of study and assist you along the way in any way I can. As a father, I would want to dissuade you, protect you. But, as the father of a son who soon will be graduating as a Second Lieutenant and serving who knows where in the world, the thought of his needing aid and comfort and finding them in the care of a nurse like you gives me some consolation."

"Thank you, sir. I will approach nurse's training with diligent effort."

"I have no doubt about that, Nancy. I'll stay abreast of your progress. Also, I'll consult with the director of the nursing program about any credits you may have that will apply to the requirements for graduation." He handed her the signed form. "Just give this to Miss Gains. She'll tell you how to proceed from here."

Nancy noted he no longer referred to her as "Miss Hodge." For whatever reason, that personal reference made her feel even more at peace with her decision. She had no idea what might lie ahead, other than her chosen pathway with its challenges and the proving of her courage and faith.

Chapter 31

Nancy determined she would retreat to her secluded spot in the library to look over the course requirements for the nursing program. She hoped she would be a few courses ahead with her completed credits. She had to wait three years before enlistment age for the Corps, but if she finished her nurses' training before then, she could get her license and practice—at least gain some experience Stateside.

"Miss Hodge, haven't you finished your studying this quarter? You seem to be digging deep into that material." Nancy looked up to see Jeffrey Langston and remembered the tentative date he had mentioned those many weeks back—before the world was turned upside down and backward beyond belief.

"Oh, no, Mr. Langston, I was just looking over the requirements for the nursing program. I have changed my course of study." Nancy was a bit surprised when Jeffrey Langston pulled a chair from the table and sat opposite her. *Perhaps*, she thought, *he's now more at ease, since 'fraternizing' is no longer forbidden.*

"No pre-med?" he asked.

"Medical school is in my future, I trust, but I can get into nursing much sooner. If this war is still going on, when I'm of age, I want to join the Army Nurse Corps."

"That's an admirable goal, Miss Hodge. I am scheduled to report for duty in a few weeks myself. My educational background should have put me in OCS with an aim toward some specialized technical area. But I fear that when the recruiter heard the word "chemistry," he just ticked 'chemical warfare.'" He added, "By the way, may I call you Nancy now?"

Nancy smiled at his new attempt at familiarity, but her response was tinged with sadness, at the thought of this gentle man's being assigned such a dangerous and threatening occupation. "Sure, she said, if I may call you Jeffrey."

"Well, even better, just call me Jeff. My friends do, and I hope you will consider yourself among them."

"Okay, thanks, Jeff." She laughed: "My brother calls me Nut Jar. You may not call me that."

"Hmm...interesting," he grinned. "One brother?"

"Yep, and that one's enough," she quipped. "No, just kidding. My brother and I are close, in age and in relationship. He's enlisting in the Army. I can't go with him, but I can study to be a nurse and help others like him, who may need care and comfort." Nancy's words broke with emotion before she finished her sentence.

"You love him very much," Jeff observed. "I'm sure he will be proud of your decision."

"Well, I'm very proud of him," she said.

"Any sisters?" he continued.

"No, just my brother and I."

"Changing the subject, Nancy, and returning to a brief exchange we had many weeks ago. Would you like to have lunch with me today? Officially, you are no longer in my lab class, so my asking you is copacetic, as they say. Are you familiar with the Dynamo Diner?"

"Oh, yes, my brother Hank and his friends enjoy going there. I've never been myself."

"Well, if today is good for you, I can introduce you to the best hamburger you've ever tasted. If you're not free now, I can come back later. Or, another option is just, 'Thanks, but no thanks.'"

"Well, I'll pass on the third option," she smiled. "But no need to come back. Just let me gather up my things." Nancy was surprised at the ease with which the plan was made and the sense of comfort she felt with Jeff.

For a few minutes, Nancy and Jeff strolled along the sidewalk in comfortable silence. She wondered how she could enjoy such a beautiful day—cool, a bit breezy, but sunny, when the burdens of suffering and death, hatred and thirst for revenge, filled the hearts of so many in the world. Acrid fumes and suffocating smoke darkened both skies and souls—remnants of destruction and devastation issuing from hearts "having no hope, and without God in the world," as she recalled the Scripture.

Jeff broke the silence: "'A penny for your thoughts,' as they say."

"Oh, excuse me, I drifted away. I was thinking about how beautiful this day is. Two new friends, strolling along, about to enjoy some good food, while so many people are suffering after Pearl Harbor—and all those other places that were attacked. The world seems so strange to me now."

"Well, perhaps, this is our calm before storms that may touch us in ways we'd rather not anticipate. When I knew I would be serving soon, I thought about all the 'What ifs'—and they were mostly unpleasant. So, I decided I'd think about the 'What nows.'"

"The 'What nows'?" Nancy questioned with a laugh.

"Yes. What do I want to do now?" He grinned: "I want to go see if Nancy Hodge is in the library. What do I want to do now? I want to ask her to have lunch with me. What do I want to do now? I want to enjoy today, this beautiful day, for we don't know how many more there will be. What do I want to do now?" Jeff stopped and pointed at the sign above the door. "Well, since we have arrived at our

destination, I want us to enjoy some delicious hamburgers."

Nancy leaned back in her chair and declared,
"That hamburger was the best I've ever had!" She
pushed the basket with remaining fries toward Jeff
and said, "I hope you can finish these. I can't possi-
bly, but they're too good to waste."

Jeff pulled the basket toward him. "I think I
can prevent any waste. My mother says I am a bot-
tomless pit." With a sound rap on the bottle, he
drenched the fries with ketchup.

"Do we need to ask for another bottle of
ketchup?" Nancy teased.

"What now?" he asked with a grin, then answered, "I am going to enjoy my ketchup without re-
gard to any judgment on your part."

Nancy laughed, "No judgment intended. I
guess I hadn't figured Mr. Langston for a ketchup
kind of guy."

"And pray tell, what is a 'ketchup kind of
guy'?"

"Well, let me see—I guess my brother,
Hank—I call him 'Jug Head'—is a 'ketchup kind of
guy'—rough and tumble, clowning, tree-climbing—
you get the idea. The picture's just strange: 'Mr.
Langston,' chemist—white lab coat, safety glasses,

Bunsen burner, chemical reactions, whopping a bottle of ketchup to douse a few measly fries."

"Hmm," he teased, "not only judgmental but with preconceptions about those of us of scientific disposition." He swirled the last fry in the puddle of ketchup in the basket and popped it in his mouth. I believe the Good Book says, 'Judge not according to the appearance.'"

"Forgive me," Nancy laughed again, "I stand corrected."

"I was rather rough and tumble as a boy," he defended himself. "In fact, Mother tells me I was destined to be a chemist. I was always coming up with new 'experiments,' mixing this and that, sometimes coming up with some horrific smells, even the occasional burst of fireworks."

Remembering the time, Nancy looked at her watch. "Jeff, this has been such a nice lunch. Thanks so much for the invitation. I never thought 'Mr. Langston' could be so entertaining. Honestly, I had you pegged as a rather shy egghead."

"Well, truth be told, I am comfortable in that role. And I did feel shy around you when our relationship was student-teacher, rather than friend-friend. And, more than that, the 'What now?' of each new day precludes wasting time on backwardness. Carpe diem!"

"Well, Jeff, thanks again. I guess I'd better run. I'm catching an earlier bus today," Nancy said, as she picked up her bag.

"Oh, sure. I don't want to cause you to miss it." He stood and reached to pull her chair from the table. "Uh…Nancy, perhaps, it's rather bold and premature to offer, but I would be happy to give you a lift. My car is in the staff lot, and I can have you home before the bus, with all those stops it will make."

"Oh, Jeff, there's no need for you to …"

"I know," he interjected. "But, frankly, it's another 'What now?' Now, I want to spend some more time with my new friend. Would your parents mind?"

"I don't think so, as long as you come in and meet my mother—so she'll know you're not some mad scientist who's a threat to kidnap me and take me to your laboratory!" she joked.

"I'll put on my best egghead persona, just for your mother, okay?"

Chapter 32

Eliza was reviewing the article Hailey had just returned to her. How thankful she was for Hailey's skill in editing and for knowing exactly what Eliza was trying to say, even when Eliza didn't say it very well. As she read, Eliza was reminded of the young girl she had been—fiercely independent—stubborn, her mother would have said. *Poor mother*, she thought, *now I understand. So hard to let children go out into a world that's so threatening.* Eliza returned the article to its folder, placed her elbows on it, and rested her face on her clenched hands. She and Josh had cried together and prayed together: Hank would be completing his graduation requirements early, and they would give him permission to enlist, as they had agreed. Again came the recurring thought she could not verbalize: *Oh, how I pray something will prevent his having to go.*

The knock at the door roused Eliza from her concern, and she saw Nancy's face peering through the side panel of glass flanking the door. Eliza opened the door, saying, "Why, Nancy, I didn't expect you home so soon." Seeing Jeffrey, she added, "Oh, hello, there!"

Jan Dearman

"Mom, hope you don't mind, but this is Jeffrey Langston. He gave me a ride home. I didn't want to burst in on you with a visitor, so I knocked."

"Come in, come in, Jeffrey." Eliza allowed them to enter the hallway, then extended her hand to Nancy's guest. "I'm Eliza Hodge. Pleased to meet you. If I'm not mistaken, you've been Nancy's lab instructor."

"Yes, ma'am, that's right. I hope you don't mind my giving Nancy a ride home. I thought I could spare her all those bus stops. She could have a little more time this afternoon to enjoy her freedom."

"Why, don't mind at all. Very considerate of you. Won't you come in and tell me how this daughter of mine has been conducting herself as a student?"

"Thank you, Mrs. Hodge, maybe five minutes," Jeff replied.

"Jeff has to report for Army duty in a few weeks. His mother wants to be with him as much as possible now that classes are over for the semester," Nancy explained.

"Oh, to be sure. I understand completely," Eliza agreed. "Come, have a seat," Eliza motioned them toward the divan in the living room. "Can I get you something to drink?"

"Thank you, ma'am, but nothing for me," Jeff responded.

"Nancy, how about you?" her mother asked.

"No, thanks, Mom. Jeff and I just had lunch at the Dynamo Diner—you know, the place Hank has been with Leigh and Cassie and Les. It's just as good as he said—great hamburgers."

Eliza sat in the nearby armchair. "So, Jeff, how has Nancy been doing in her lab work?"

"Well, ma'am, her grades have been excellent, but we do fear tuition will increase next year to pay for all the equipment she's broken or blown up."

Eliza's concern and surprise turned to laughter when Nancy retorted, "Why, Jeffrey Langston, you know that's not true!"

"No, ma'am," he chuckled, "I was just kidding. She's done excellent work. I'm sure she will do an outstanding job in the medical field—or in whatever endeavor she pursues."

"That's good to hear, Jeffrey. I know my husband will be pleased also." Eliza proceeded with care: "So, you are enlisting in a few weeks?"

"No, ma'am, I'm reporting for duty. I was twenty-one shortly after Pearl Harbor. I wanted to go ahead and enlist, in hope of having more input about my occupational specialty."

"Well, Jeff, please be assured we will keep you in our prayers," Eliza promised. "And we will remember your parents, also. I know how difficult this must be for them."

"I only have my mother, Mrs. Hodge. My dad died when I was young. But I will tell her about your kindness in thinking of her." Jeffrey stood and said, "I really hate to cut short our visit, but I'd better be running along. It was a pleasure to meet you, Mrs. Hodge."

Eliza stood and responded, "And you, Jeffrey. I hope you'll come again sometime when you can meet the rest of our family. Eliza waited while Nancy followed Jeff to the door.

"Thanks again, Jeff, for lunch and for bringing me home."

"Thank you for keeping me company today," he responded.

"I hope you'll drop by and let us see you before you report for duty," Nancy added, as she opened the door and went out on the porch with Jeff.

Before starting down the front steps, he turned to ask, "Well, what now, Miss Hodge? Now I think I'll go check my calendar and see if I can arrange a few more times to share hamburgers with my new friend. I'm sure there won't be any Dynamo burgers in the mess hall where I'm going."

"That sounds like a fine idea," Nancy agreed. "Maybe some evening you and your friend can expand your circle to include a couple of 'ketchup kind of guys' and their girlfriends. It would be fun to see if they can guess you're an egghead scientist."

Jeff laughed and proceeded down the steps with a wave and "Have a good afternoon."

Eliza met Nancy as she came back into the hallway. "Well, that was a surprise!"

"Well, I was a little surprised too. He found me in the library and asked me to lunch. I know he's thinking about his upcoming service and wants to enjoy his life now as much as he can before the Army is controlling it."

Eliza commented: "I can understand that. He seems like a nice young man. He obviously likes you. Think you'll be seeing him again?"

"He indicated I might," Nancy smiled, then added, "He's polite and intelligent. Professor Albright seems to have a lot of confidence in him. Unfortunately, Jeff's degrees are putting him in the field of chemical warfare. That has to be dangerous."

Eliza simply sighed, "Oh, me," shook her head, and moved toward her desk.

"Mom, are you busy, or can I talk to you about something?" Nancy asked as she returned to sit on the divan.

"Never too busy for you, dear." Eliza responded and sat again in the armchair.

Nancy focused her thoughts and then announced: "Mom, I have changed my course of study to nursing. I plan to finish my training in three years, perhaps less. Then, if this war is still going on, I want to join the Army Nurse Corps. I hope you and Dad will understand and support me in this decision."

Eliza processed the information for a few seconds, then asked, "What about your plans for medical school?"

"I'm young. There will be plenty of time for medical school, and nurses' training will give me a head start." Noting the anxiety in her mother's face, Nancy continued: "Mom, Hank and Les are planning to serve. Perhaps they or others like them will need comfort and care. I want to be able to do that for them."

Nancy waited in silence for her mother to respond.

"As I see it, you are an adult and must make your own decision about this. If you like, I can tell your father about the change in your plan. He may talk to you about it, or he may just accept it without comment. I don't think I'll mention the Nurse Corps. That's three years down the road. Maybe this terrible war will be behind us by then."

Chapter 33

March 18, 1942
To Whom It May Concern:

This is to certify that I am principal of North Side High School, and John Henry "Hank" Hodge has been a student at this institution for three years.

His class work here has been of superior quality. In fact, the courses he has completed and the grades he has achieved on required examinations make it possible for him to graduate early, with highest honors. At the age of seventeen, he will complete his junior year in May of this year.

In addition to academic excellence, his qualities of leadership have won him an enviable place among his fellow students. His demonstrated attributes of character and trustworthiness cause both instructors and students to place utmost confidence in him and to predict for him a bright future.

It gives me pleasure to commend him to anyone who may need his services.

Yours very cordially,
Arthur L. McConnell, Principal

Hank tried to assess his father's reaction as he read the recommendation, then passed it to Eliza, who, having completed her reading, refolded the document and returned it to the official envelope Josh had laid before them after dinner. "Well, Hank, it seems you have kept up your end of the bargain. Do you agree, Josh?"

"Yes," he paused, "so it seems." Josh turned the envelope to face himself and smoothed its edges while he considered his response. "Son, I will be a man of my word. When the time comes, I will sign whatever papers you need to give my permission to complete your enlistment."

Hank said, "Thanks, Dad."

Nancy had sat in silence wondering if her father knew about her change of course, about the possibility of Army nursing, when Josh added: "Unfortunately, it seems both our children are of a military mindset. Independence and daring—do those characteristics remind you of anyone, my dear?" he asked, turning to smile at Eliza. "I should have known when I married you I would likely have to deal with offspring like their mother," he teased, taking Eliza's hand. Josh looked at Hank, then at Nancy: "Children, I am sad and fearful when I think of the challenges and dangers that may lie ahead for you. But I want you to know I am also so proud of the man and woman you are. I pray God will shield you from harm—or heal you from injury if that should happen. And I pray, when this awful war is behind us, we all may still be here, together at this table, as a family, to thank God for allowing it to be so."

Nancy moved to her father's chair to give him a hug and a kiss on the cheek. She turned to mouth a silent "Thank you" toward her mother. When Hank stood to leave the table, he approached his father and folded him in his arms. They embraced as if neither could let go.

Chapter 34
April 1942

Jeff opened the door to the Dynamo and said, "Wow, this place is jumping this evening! That's the correct term, isn't it?"

Nancy laughed and raised her volume: "I'm not sure. But, if jumping means noisy, it applies." The Andrews Sisters were blasting "Bugle Boy" from the juke box, as Nancy led the way through the diner. "Hank said they would be in the back at a table for six where it's a little more private. Maybe we can actually hear each other. Oh, there they are!"

"Hey, Nut Jar and the Egg Head! The gang's all here!" Hank exclaimed.

Nancy and Jeff sat at one side of the table, across from Leigh and Cassie, with Hank and Les at the ends near their girls.

"Jeff, this is my brother, Hank, better known as Jug Head, of course. This is Leigh Burkhart. Leigh has taken pity on poor old Jug Head—kind of reminds you of 'Beauty and the Beast,' doesn't it?" Hank, in clown mode, displayed his best fiendish face.

Jeff nodded with a chuckle and accepted Leigh's outstretched hand. "Hi, Leigh."

Nancy continued: "This is Cassie Hawthorne—she goes with Les—Les Thompson, captain and star of the North Side football team. He's soon to be Private Thompson when called up for duty in a few weeks, perhaps with Jug Head, if Hank's paperwork is processed and he can pass the required intelligence test."

They all laughed as Hank replied, "Ha! Early graduate just like old Nut Jar!" He tapped his head: "She didn't get all the brains in the family—or all of the looks."

Jeff shook hands with Cassie and Les, as Nancy finished, "Everyone, this is Jeff Langston, also reporting for service."

Les observed, "Well, this is beginning to look like a going away party."

"Surely we'll get in a few more get-togethers before that one," Hank declared.

"Well, this is going to have to be it for me," Jeff informed them. "I just got notice today I'm to report for induction next Wednesday. If I pass the final physical, I'm on my way."

"Do you know where you're going?" Les asked.

"I think Camp Gordon—Chemical Battalion," Jeff replied.

"Whew," Hank whistled, "heavy stuff."

Leigh interrupted, "Girls, I don't know about you, but I'd like to declare all war talk off limits this evening."

"I'll second that motion," Nancy agreed.

"And I'll third it," said Cassie. "As far as I'm concerned, if you guys want to talk Army, just go find yourselves another table."

Speaking up, Les asked, "What about it, guys? You want to go talk war or stay here peacefully with three dishy ladies?"

"It's dishy ladies for me," Jeff announced.

"I have to agree with Jeff. He's the man with the degrees," Hank grinned and winked at his sister.

"What can I get you guys—the usual?" the waiter inquired as he passed their table.

"What about it, everybody—hamburgers and cokes?" Les asked. He waited for their assent and said, "That'll do it, Vic." Les whispered something to Cassie, and she smiled and nodded, before Les said: "Nancy and Jeff, Cassie and I have an announcement. We are going to treat everyone to ice cream sodas for dessert, to celebrate the fact that we eloped night before last. We are now Mr. and Mrs. Lester G. Thompson, Jr. Hank and Leigh were our witnesses."

After a moment's silence to process the news, Nancy erupted with questions: "What? Hank, you knew about this? Cassie, do your parents know?

Where did you go? Cassie, what about school—you've got another year?"

"Whoa, Nut Jar," Hank ordered, "one question at a time!"

Cassie held Les' hand while she answered: "This year will be no problem, since Hank and Leigh are sworn to secrecy around the school," she grinned, "and then I'll finish and graduate later when I can. Right now, we're going to stay in the basement apartment of Les' parents' house. When he goes to his duty station, I'll see about finding a place near the base and stay there till he has to deploy. And, yes, my parents know. We told them our plans a few days ago. They said they wished things could be different—that there was time for a big wedding and friends and family." She paused. "But they understand the world has changed, hopefully, not for long. We want to be together now and make the most of every day we have."

"Leigh and I went with them," Hank teased, "so we could see just what's involved in this elopement thing."

"Hank, you two aren't thinking of…" Nancy started.

"Oh no, sis, we were just the support troops—and scouts," he laughed. "Don't worry, Nut Jar. I'm kidding. Leigh wants to graduate, and I want to be 'gainfully employed,' as they say, before we get hitched."

"I've been working part-time at the hardware store," Les added, "so we can have a little something to hold us until I start getting pay and spousal support from the Army. Our parents have been understanding—worried some, I know, but trying to help as they can."

"Les called me up the other afternoon and asked me if I'd stand up with him," Hank proceeded with the account. "And Cassie called Leigh and asked her to be the maid of honor. Les had made arrangements with the Justice of the Peace in Trenton, so we headed down there."

"I'm glad we're not superstitious," Cassie added. "Just as Les said, 'I do,' the cuckoo clock on the wall behind the JP sounded—'Cuckoo, Cuckoo!'"

"Yeah, Cass," said Hank, "that was to let you know the deal was sealed and you had just married a cuckoo!"

Les continued, "Thanks, bud! Yeah, we had a good laugh with the Justice of the Peace. He said he'd never before had that thing go off during a ceremony. I'll consider it an omen of happiness—starting married life with a good laugh." He hugged Cassie close and kissed her cheek.

Vic had brought their round of drinks while Les was speaking. When he set the soda in front of Les, the waiter announced, "Les, I heard you say you got married, so the drinks for everybody are on the house and the food for you and your new Mrs."

"Thanks, Vic! That sure is nice of you. We're not making a public announcement just yet, so keep it under wraps a while." Les continued, "We've had a lot of fun here at the Diner and hope we'll be regulars for a long time to come—maybe bring our kids here for their first hamburgers," Les suggested.

Vic responded, "Well, if you do, the first burger for each child will be on the house."

Les joked, "We plan on a big family. You may need to set a limit."

"Just bring them in one at a time—not all ten at once," Vic laughed.

Jeff, who had been observing, tapped his glass with his fork and announced: "I know I'm the new guy at the table, but I think it's only fitting that we raise a toast to Mr. and Mrs. Les Thompson and wish them a long and happy married life."

"Here, here," agreed Hank, "and ten beautiful children—girls as pretty as their mother, boys as strong as their father, and all of them as intelligent as…." he paused, "their mother, of course."

Leigh had only smiles for her friends, but the light of her expression hid weightier thoughts and troubling, if humbling, understanding of herself and her parents. For a few days now, Leigh had been

188

forced to consider her impending adulthood. She had sought to fulfill her duty as maid of honor with maturity and attention to detail, but all the while she felt a stranger, thrust into a new world of challenges and responsibilities for which she was ill-prepared. Cassie seemed so confident and brave, forging into a fog—or, perhaps, a cloud of smoke, beyond which ...well, no one could say. In her thoughts, Cassie became Rose Burkhart at seventeen—in love, adventurous, hanging all her heart and hope on the life of Jack Stanfield, never considering the possibility that death could interrupt so perfect a picture as theirs. Leigh realized her mother had been alone, fearful, in a cloud of darkness, into which Charles appeared as part of Jack's remaining light—along with Jack's child, for whom she had become solely responsible. For Charles Burkhart, a deep, silent man, tortured by ghosts, to whom Jack had been a rare, true friend, Rose must have seemed a candle in the night. *So strange*, Leigh thought, *Jack Stanfield brought them together and then kept them apart for all those years.*

Nancy joined the others in the laughter; but her thoughts were racing ahead to tearful departures, the sights and sounds of conflict, the threats of injury, the possibility of death, and futures and families formed only in dreams but never in reality. Even though Hank's enlistment papers were filed, and she had changed her course of study, only with the marriage of Cassie and Les did Nancy realize the life she was living would bear little resemblance to the life that would be. Cassie and Les, though young, perhaps understood better than any of them at the table, the preciousness of the transient vapor of life and time. She wondered if they could fully comprehend that, in the days and weeks ahead, they might be thrust into a strange, new world, in which established norms and ideals—everything they held dear, would be overshadowed by uncertainty, threat of destruction, quest for survival, and a desire to return to an irretrievable place existent only in memory?

Chapter 35

Eliza sat in the front porch swing in the soft breeze of a glorious morning, her thoughts in sharp disharmony to the spring melody of blue sky, songbirds, and rose blossoms. Her children had entered an adult world that her generation had left suffering and scarred, then had renovated sufficiently only to be destroyed and darkened again by man's insatiate greed. She kept telling herself that Nancy and Hank now were adults who needed freedom to meet challenges of their own choosing. She tried to remember the feeling of wanting to prove she had courage, strength, and true convictions that motivated willpower, action, and progress toward whatever goal she had set for herself. *Such high ideals*, she thought with a smile. But noble goals seemed elusive, the road progressing toward them littered with mangled bodies and broken dreams. *Morgan and Maddie—so tragic! Could I ever have their strength? And Josh—can he survive the stress?*

Eliza's clouded reverie was interrupted by the sound of an approaching car turning into their driveway. Jeff Langston, the tall, slim young man with the flashing smile that warmed Eliza's heart, closed the car door and began his ascent up the walkway to the porch steps.

"Well, good morning, Mr. Langston!" Eliza greeted him.

Josh turned toward her voice. "Oh, Mrs. Hodge, I didn't see you there in the swing. How are you this fine morning?"

"I'm well. Just trying to let the sunshine and breeze whisk away the dust and cobwebs."

She continued: "And what brings you over here, as if I don't know," she chuckled.

"Well, ma'am, I just wanted to see Nancy once more before I leave tomorrow. I hope she's home and won't mind my dropping by."

Eliza rose as she laughed, "I'll see if she's receiving guests. You take my seat in the swing—it's nice and warm."

He responded, "Yes, ma'am. Thank you, ma'am."

The screened door slammed behind Eliza as she entered the doorway to the hall and called up the stairway, "Nancy, Jeff is here to see you!" She waited before repeating her announcement: "Nancy, you have a guest on the front porch!"

Nancy's bedroom door opened, and she asked, "Jeff is here?"

"Yes, dear. He wants to see you before he leaves tomorrow. Are you presentable?" Eliza asked.

"Oh, sure, Mom. I was just reorganizing my room a bit. Let me run a brush through my hair, and I'll be right down."

Jan Dearman

Nancy knew the time would come to say goodbye to Jeff. *Such a dear, sweet man*, she thought. He had become a good friend, and she found all her moments with him comfortable camaraderie. There were serious, private moments, when she prayed for him, as she did for Hank and Les. But there were so many men just like them, and she knew they could not all return home as they had left— whole, healthy…alive.

Nancy checked herself in the mirror—green-checked blouse and dungarees, a dash of lipstick— *good enough for a surprise house call.* She bounced down the stairs and out the door, allowing it to slam behind her.

Lounging as he swayed in the swing, Jeff laughed and observed: "You and your mother are a bit rambunctious—she slams going in, and you slam coming out."

Nancy replied, "Well, what can I say? We are on the move!" Approaching the swing, Nancy asked, "Do you think you might make room for me, or would you like to just lie down there and take a nap?"

"Oh, I might be able to squeeze up to one side," he replied, as he straightened himself and moved to make room. "Your posterior diametric measurement is rather narrow."

"Only a man of your intelligence and scientific background could get away with saying something like that and not get his head knocked off!" she laughed, as she took her place next to him. She paused before continuing: "I'm really glad you came by. I was hoping to see you before you report tomorrow."

He responded after a moment's silence: "I wanted to say goodbye. These couple of months have been so great—so much fun. I'm glad I've been free of my Egghead persona for a while and able to enjoy life—because of you, and your family and friends."

"We have had some good times, haven't we?" Nancy agreed. "If I must eat a Dynamo burger without you, I will be thinking of you with every bite," she teased, as she bumped him with her shoulder.

Another pause, and Jeff went on: "Nancy, I have a couple of favors to ask."

"Well, sure, Jeff, whatever I can do—feed your dog, water your plants…" Then Nancy noticed Jeff's expression—serious, concerned, needy. "I'm sorry, Jeff. It's not time to kid around…but I guess I'm fearful of the time to be serious."

Nancy felt her resolve to be light-hearted fading, as he spoke: "Nancy, I'd like to ask you to visit my mother once in a while—or call her. She has a few friends, but no one who would be as helpful or dependable as you if she really needed assistance or comfort. It's going to be hard on her when I leave. I'm all she's had for so long, and since I've been grown, she's become more dependent on having me around. I think just being able to talk to you occasionally would be good for her."

"Sure, Jeff, I'll do what I can to help. Tell her I'm going to be in touch—perhaps arrange a visit this week. These first days may be especially tough."

"Thanks," Jeff responded, taking Nancy's hand, "I thought you would help. That eases my mind some. And the other favor—may I write to you, and will you write back?"

"Why, Jeff, you'd better write to me! And, of course, I'll write to you! I guess you'll have to write first, so I'll have your address. I'll write at least once a week, maybe more, depending on my school load. Just think of me in my cozy little library nook with my stack of nursing texts, from which I'll take an occasional break to write a paragraph to update my old chem lab instructor."

Jeff paused. "Maybe a third favor? Would you have a picture of yourself I could take with me? I know we're just friends, but you never know when I might need to see a friendly face."

Nancy squeezed Jeff's hand and replied, "I think I might find one. Hang on, I'll be back in a sec." The screen door slammed again as Nancy hurried inside and bounded the stairs two steps at a time. From her desk she retrieved the photos her father had taken during their last family gathering on the river. She remembered there was one of her she liked: a candid snap taken at the big oak tree had caught her with a natural smile and her curls under control. She'd like for Jeff to remember her like that. Nancy bounded back down and out to the porch. "Here's this one—about the best I've got. I hate to have my picture taken."

Jeff took the photo from her hand and looked at it for a moment. "Almost as pretty as you are in person," he said. "Thanks." He put the picture in his shirt pocket and patted it, saying, "When I can, I'll write to tell you about all the strange, foreign places where your face has been seen and admired."

Nancy sat again next to Jeff. "Well, in that first letter to me, I expect to find a picture of you."

Jeff looked into his shirt pocket and retrieved a second photo. "I just happen to have one with me— taken in the chem lab. I rather like it. I may have been in the Egghead environment, but I think I look rather dashing and non-ovoid."

Taking the snap, Nancy assessed it. She admitted, "Yes, not Egghead at all—very handsome, very photogenic."

For a few moments they lingered in the swing, with no words, only the breeze and birdsongs.

196

"I should go," Jeff said. "I have to pack and tie up some loose ends with Mother—see that she's clear on finances, rationing, other things I've helped her handle."

Nancy replied, "Sure, I understand, Jeff. Thanks for coming by." They stood and moved toward the porch steps. Nancy added, "Just remember I'll be thinking about you and praying for you every day—and hoping to see you again as soon as possible."

Jeff started down the steps, then turned and took Nancy's hand and pressed it to his lips, his eyes closed as if in petition. Then, he looked at her and declared, "Oh, yes, Nancy, I will see you again as soon as possible." He studied her hand before declaring, "What now, Miss Hodge?" He pulled her toward him and kissed her. After a few seconds, he released her and whispered, "What now? Now, I can leave with even more precious memories of my lab student and friend."

Nancy remained motionless, except for silent tears betraying her emotions. She watched Jeff as he went toward the car. She snapped a mental photo of his customary action of brushing back the hair from his brow and pushing the glasses up the bridge of his nose. She saw his last smiling glance and salute above the open car door. She watched as he backed out of the driveway. She was stunned by the sudden revelation. *How did I not know? Why did I not feel it or see it? Dear God, please bring him back to me!*

The screen door slammed, and Eliza said, "I heard the car. Jeff has left?" Nancy turned toward her mother, who noticed her tears and asked, "Are you all right, dear?"

"No, Mother, I'm not." Nancy moved into her mother's arms. "Mother, he kissed me. I just realized I love him, and I may never see him again."

Eliza's thoughts returned to the sixteen-year-old she was, sitting with Josh Hodge in the shade of the big oak tree. She was so young and inexperienced, so startled by the first unexpected kiss she could only stammer, "I need to get back to work. I'll be seeing you." She had left Josh alone on the rock. Her romantic daydreams suddenly had taken substance, but one simple kiss had confounded her, and she had fled back to the familiarity and security of Sugar and the Trail.

Now, all these years later, her daughter was experiencing her own new awakening—to love and to the pain that might accompany it. Eliza remembered the weeks of waiting and wondering if Josh would survive being shot in Cincinnati and, if he did, would he return to her—an immature, tomboyish girl, filled with new womanly feelings.

"Come sit." Her arm wrapped around Nancy, Eliza moved her daughter back to the swing. They swayed in silence while Nancy rested her head on her mother's shoulder, and Eliza stroked her hair. She thought before reminiscing: "I remember the first time your father kissed me—the time I knew—I really knew that I didn't want a life without him." She paused. "He was older, and I could hardly believe he was interested in me. There I was in your Uncle John's cut-down Levi's, smelling of the outdoors and saddle leather." She smiled. "But here we are, nearly thirty years later, and our life has been so blessed—with you and Hank and a love that has withstood pain and loss." She sighed. "We don't know what challenges lie ahead. Surely, dying and death will be a big hurdle for us—but living after death may be even more challenging for the one left behind." Eliza's voice trailed to a whisper.

Nancy raised her head to look at Jeff's photograph. "He's not at all what I thought when he was my lab instructor. He was proper, polite, obviously intelligent—scientific," Nancy chuckled. "But then, when lab was behind us, he also was open and warm, and we were comfortable with each other—we made each other laugh." Nancy rested her head again on Eliza. "Mother, what do I do?"

Eliza prayed for the right words before speaking. "Well, dear, I dare say Jeff is feeling like you do—in love, hopeful, but fearful of the future. We only can see the moment at hand, especially in these troublesome times. Write him encouraging letters. Tell him about your studies. Make him smile, even laugh at times when he reads about your goings-on. Make him feel there is a normal life waiting for him when he comes back, and you will be there to see he enjoys every day in it. Above all, be patient and pray—and stay busy."

Nancy sat erect as she wiped her eyes. "Oh, Mother, why didn't you warn me this love business will take more strength and courage than being an Army nurse?"

Eliza added, "And more than hefting mail bags and riding all those miles on the Trail!" Measuring her words, Eliza continued: "But love is the great motivator for everything worthwhile. It will give you gratitude for the blessings and patience for the challenges—and an open heart and welcoming arms when 'Jeffrey Comes Marching Home Again.'"

Nancy laughed as she stood. "Well, back to my room reorganizing. 'Stay busy.' Maybe I can re-organize my brain after the whirlwind that's going on in my head." Nancy opened the screened door, then turned and said, "Mom, thanks. I love you."

Eliza replied, "I love you, too, dear." She noted the care with which Nancy closed the door, and she was unable to detect the sound of feet ascending

Jan Dearman

the stairs. She closed her eyes: *Please, God, help these young people find their way through this dark and dangerous world.*

Chapter 36
May 1942

Order to Report for Induction: No. 12733
To John Henry Hodge:

Having submitted yourself to a local board composed of your neighbors for the purpose of determining your availability for training and service in the armed forces of the United States, you are hereby notified that you have now been selected for training and service in the Land or Naval Forces.

You will, therefore, report to the local board at 1:30 P. M. on the 15th day of June 1942.

You will there be examined, and, if accepted for training and service, you will then be inducted into the service.

Persons reporting to the induction station in some instances may be rejected for physical or other reasons. It is well to keep this in mind in arranging your affairs, to prevent any undue hardship if you are rejected at the induction station.

Willful failure to report promptly to this local board is a violation of the Selective Service Training and Service Acts of 1940...

Hank and Les sat on the top step of the Thompsons' front porch and compared the notices they had received. The breezy beauty of the spring day would imprint the memory of the moment and the reality of the future for the remainder of their days.

"How is Cassie doing?" Hank asked.

"About like you'd expect—brave, but lots of quiet tears," Les responded. "It's all real now—no more playing Army and being some kind of save-the-day heroes."

"Yeah," Hanks agreed, "maybe bullet holes, body bags, or one boot wonders."

"No talk like that around the girls, Junior Bud," Les warned.

"Aw, give me a break—I've got more sense than that," Hank protested. "I probably shouldn't have even said that to you, but guess I just want to be up-front about it. Can't deny things can happen—just have to be trained and prepared to get through without thinking about what's on the other side."

Les broke a period of silence: "Well, we've got to make the most of the time we have left. I want to spend as much time with Cassie as I can, but maybe we can work in some guy time."

Hank was pensive, then said, "I've got to go out to the river to see my family there before we report. Want to make an afternoon of it and do a little fishing with the cousins, just us guys?"

"Yeah, that'd be good. Maybe we can take the girls and let them visit for a while with your aunt and her family?"

"Aunt Lindy would like that. I'll check with Leigh to see if that works for her." Hank laughed, "She needs to get to know the river folk if she's going to be part of the family someday."

"They're good people," Les grinned, "salt of the earth,' as they say, but likely a new experience for your city-bred Leigh."

Hank frowned. "Then there's Aunt Dovey— I'll have to prepare Leigh for her."

"Oh, yeah," Les agreed. "I forgot about her. She might be a little scary on first meeting without a heads-up."

"Oh, Dovey's mostly harmless—more a threat to herself than anyone else. But she's hefty and strong, especially when one of her fits is coming on. It's the kisses she wants to give that kind of makes you want to take to the mountains."

"But, you know," Les observed, "I've noticed she sometimes can remember things and say things that let you know there's still some light left on in her brain."

"Well, Mom says she was about like Nut Jar when she was little—really smart—until the accident.

Even now, she still plays the piano sometimes for the Baptist mission out there, and she never had a lesson. The brain's an interesting thing." After a moment of introspection, Hank added, "We've just got to keep our brains intact. As long as we can think straight and act right, we can do without a part here or there."

"Like I said, no talk like that around the girls, Bud." He tousled Hank's hair. "They've just got to think of us as two handsome dudes in uniforms marching off with the Andrews Sisters singing 'Bugle Boy' in the background."

Chapter 37

"Aunt Lindy, you remember Les and Cassie, don't you?" Hank asked as they entered the front door.

"Yes, I sure do," Lindy replied. "Good to see y'all again." Before Hank could continue, she added, "And this must be Miss Leigh. My sister's told me so much about you—'pretty and smart,' I believe she said."

"Thank you, Mrs. Sexton. I'm pleased to meet you," responded Leigh, as she looked for similarities between Hank's mother and her younger sister and noted Lindy's chestnut hair, streaked with the light blonde of aging, in contrast to Eliza's silvered dark tresses. Rather than wearing fashionable waves and updos, both sisters maintained their long locks in coiled braids that emphasized the heritage of their attractive features, dark eyes and gently aquiline noses.

"Come in and make yourself at home." Lindy continued. "I'll let Byrd know you're here, and Louise and Tom should be on their way down with Dovey. She's stayed with them a while today while I cleaned the house. Later on, John and Caroline are planning on coming by."

Leigh noted "the old Sexton homestead," as Hank had described it, was neat and well-maintained. They had entered from a front porch extending the length of the structure, which faced what was once the trail Eliza and Sugar had traversed carrying the mail. At the right end of the long combination living and dining room stood an imposing fireplace with a heavy oak mantel, in front of which Leigh saw an oval mahogany table surrounded by chairs. She smiled when she was reminded of Hank's saying the occasional Sexton and Hodge family gatherings were boisterous events, mainly because so many of them were half-deaf.

"Ladies, the washroom is just down the hall," Lindy indicated a bedroom wing on the left, as she led them across the room to the back door, past the kitchen entrance on the right. They exited through a screened door to the wide, shaded, riverside porch, where Lindy had placed a picnic table with red checked oilcloth cover. Wooden benches flanked the table, and red-cushioned rockers lining the remainder of the porch waited to ensconce bodies and relax souls in the sounds of lapping water and feminine conversation. "You boys picked a fine day to fish or swim or whatever you set your mind to doing. I thought some of us might want to picnic out here later on when we eat dinner. The skeeters and flies haven't been bad lately. And, while you men are gone, we women can sit out here and enjoy the breeze while we shoot the breeze."

Les and Cassie took seats on one of the benches, Leigh sat in a rocker leaving one next to her for Hank, but he chose to lean against the rail in front of her. They watched Lindy as she walked to a corner of the porch, where an iron school bell hung from the post, and she pulled the rope tied to the crank and sounded the clanging signal. "Byrd's been in the shed getting fishing gear ready. He'll be here shortly. John's working late, so he and Caroline will have pie and coffee with us after their meal at home."

Hank said, "I haven't seen them since the holidays. I hope to see J. T. and Thomas in town before we report for duty."

Lindy responded with a sigh, "Yes, seems most of our young men have had to leave the river to find work. The old ways can't keep up with the demands—or the costs, of these modern times. Thankfully, they've found good jobs with the foundry and TNT plant that will keep them out of the battles but in the fight." She shook her head. "Such a sad time. William already has finished boot camp and is at Fort Gordon. I just take each day as it comes, try to occupy my time, and turn my cares over to the Lord. What more can a mother do?"

"Where are Rachel and Leah now?" Hank asked.

"Well, after she finished business school in Chattanooga, Rachel got a government job. Now, she's a secretary on Governor Cooper's staff in Nashville. She's not married yet—and about to be too old to be in contention," she smiled.

"Whoa," replied Hank, "she's a long way from home on the river."

Lindy laughed, "Yes, and now working with all those bureaucrats—a rose among thorns!"

They all laughed, as Lindy continued: "And Leah married a fellow she met when she went to visit her wayward cousin Rachel, and they're living in Winchester. He's a got a job in a bank, and they have their first child on the way."

The sound of footsteps coming up the porch steps was followed by Byrd's deep, mellow voice: "Well, Lindy, have you brought them all up to speed on our family near and far?"

Lindy answered, "Yes, dear. All the chicks that have scattered, it seems, except for little Louise."

Byrd extended his left hand to Les. "Good to see you again. And this must be your new missus."

Les had no time to respond before Cassie declared proudly, "Yes, sir, now Cassie Hawthorne Thompson" and displayed the gold band on her finger.

Byrd chuckled: "Well, congratulations to the groom for getting a pretty bride, and best wishes to the bride who now has to deal with a man in the house."

Byrd proceeded to Hank and wrapped his arm around him to pull him close. "So good to see you, Hank. Hope you and the family are well."

"Yes, sir, all well." Turning to Leigh, he added, "Uncle Byrd, this is my girlfriend, Leigh Burkhart."

"Pleased to meet you, Leigh. Glad you can be with us." Turning to his wife, Byrd said, "We surely won't have a shortage of pretty women around here today, will we, Lindy?" Byrd winked at the group, "Of course, I must say, my Lindy always has been the cream of any crop."

"Oh, Byrd, stop that silliness," grinned Lindy. "Tom and Louise are coming down with Dovey. How about meeting them and bringing them out to the porch?"

Hank had told Leigh about Byrd's accident in the mine all those years go. She had prepared herself to meet him with ease and normality. However, Hank also had warned her about Dovey, and she was a bit fearful of that encounter. She wanted to be warm and gracious, but Dovey was unlike anyone she had ever known. Hank had said even the family members never knew exactly what to expect with Dovey— whether she would be mild-mannered and conversational, or sullen and threatening to convulse. He also had mentioned her proclivity to kiss—even strangers. Knowing Hank might be embarrassed by his aunt, she had assured him, "Don't worry. I'll try to be ready for anything." She hoped she could react in a way that would minimize Hank's discomfort.

Byrd returned through the screened porch door, followed by red-haired Louise, her shoulder-length hair framing a face that reminded Leigh of Judy Garland. Louise's husband Tom came next—a tall, slim, dark-haired man in denim overalls and a white shirt, who seemed shy and quiet, shaking hands with the boys and just smiling and nodding at the girls. Lumbering behind them came Dovey, her corpulent body covered by a clean, blue-flowered cotton dress, her short gray page-boy hair held off her face by a matching blue barrette, and her feet shod in white socks and serviceable rubber-soled brown oxfords. Byrd finished a new round of introductions, while Leigh tried to avoid the fixed gaze Dovey had directed toward her.

"Well, you guys, who's going to the river ?" Hank asked.

"I'll take you boys in my skiff," Tom drawled. "Tied up just down the bank."

"Uncle Byrd, you want to go with us?" asked Hank.

Lindy answered, "Byrd, why don't you go along with Tom in his boat? Hank and Les can take yours. You'd enjoy getting out on the water—more than sitting around listening to us, cackling hens."

Byrd hesitated, "Well, when you put it that way." He moved toward the steps, giving Lindy a kiss on the cheek as he passed. "Men, come on. We'll pick up the gear in the shed. The back path leads to the river and our skiffs." Byrd's words trailed behind them: "We'll be looking forward to that good meal in two or three hours."

"It'll be ready and plenty. You be safe," Lindy called back.

Hank squeezed Leigh's shoulder and said, "Back soon." Les gave Cassie a quick kiss, and they followed Tom, who trailed after Byrd without comment or kiss for Louise. The women, noticing, laughed when Louise declared, "Well, that's my husband for you. They say, 'Still waters run deep,' but sometimes still waters are just still waters."

When the men had cleared the porch, floorboards creaked as Dovey moved to sit in the rocker next to Leigh. Still smiling at her, Dovey leaned toward Leigh and kissed her cheek. Leigh returned Dovey's smile and said, "Hello, Dovey. How are you today?"

Dovey's deep voice was thick in response: "Good." Leaning closer still, Dovey gently stroked Leigh's cheek with the back of her hand. "Lindy, she's a good hog."

Shock and question in her expression, Leigh looked to Lindy for explanation, while Cassie tried to restrain a burst of laughter.

"Oh, Leigh, please excuse her," Lindy explained, covering her mouth with her hand and shaking her head in embarrassment. "Dovey's eyes are sharp as an eagle's. She noticed blonde hairs on that pretty face of yours. The hairs on a hog's jowl are a sign of quality. Apparently she finds you healthy with good breeding. Please don't be insulted. In her mind that's a compliment."

Leigh laughed and said to Dovey, "Why, thank you, Dovey."

Dovey leaned back in the chair and began rocking and watching the martins swoop around their houses, perched on poles in the narrow yard between the porch and the riverside.

Lindy took a seat across from Cassie on the end of the opposite bench and continued: "When we were young girls, we had a pet pig for a while—until the pig became a hog fit for a feast." She smiled wistfully. "Dovey called him Porkypie."

Leigh tried to imagine the sisters as young girls. It was hard to picture Dovey as the precocious, joyful, musical child Eliza had described to Hank. She wondered about the woman Dovey might have become, if not for the accident that had wrung so much from her over the years.

"Well, girls, I'm going to go see about the food. If you'd like to have a snack before the men come back, I've got some fried apple pies and milk. We'll have dinner when they return. They'll likely be starved."

Cassie asked, "Can we help?"

"Sure, much appreciated," Lindy replied. "But we won't need to do anything till later—just set out the dinnerware and drinks in the kitchen. We're going to fix our own plates from the food on the stove and either sit at the table inside or picnic outside— whatever's more comfortable. Like I said, lately there seems to be just enough breeze to shoosh away the skeeters and flies."

Leigh said, "Sounds good," and leaned back in the rocker. Now more comfortable with Dovey beside her, she said, "Cassie, you ought to come and rock with us. I believe this is just about the most relaxing place I've ever been.

Cassie moved to sit in the other rocker next to Leigh. They rocked in silence until Lindy returned to the porch and directed her sister: "Dovey, how about moving over a rocker so I can sit next to Leigh?"

Dovey frowned but complied and lugged her heavy form out of one seat and plopped into the next.

"Thanks, sister." Lindy settled into the comfort of the chair and sighed, "Well, food's all ready and staying warm. Leigh, you'll be impressed—maybe concerned, when you see the chicken and dumplings Hank Hodge can put away in one meal."

"Hah, is that so? I've only seen him put away a couple of Dynamo burgers, a large order of fries, and about a half bottle of ketchup. Oh, yes—and a large chocolate soda for dessert." Their laughter faded to quietude, as they rocked in the filtered sunlight and gentle breeze.

Breaking the tranquility, Cassie asked, "Mrs. Sexton, how often do you hear from William?"

Lindy considered her response, then said, "Well, during boot camp, we didn't hear from him at all. That was difficult. But, as soon as he got to Fort Gordon, he wrote and said he'd try to send a letter every week or two. He'll let us know when he gets his overseas orders. By the time we receive that letter, he'll likely be gone. Then, we'll just have to be patient—and pray."

Cassie agreed, "Yes." She paused. "Les keeps telling me I'm strong and he trusts me to handle things here at home. But I don't know—I won't know, until he leaves and I'm alone."

"Well, I assume your parents are supportive, aren't they?" Lindy asked.

"Oh, yes, the Thompsons are as supportive as Les will allow—he wants us to be independent. But we are living in his folks' basement apartment, which only makes sense right now. They are good people, and I get along well with them, but they are so anxious. Les is their only child. I know they're worried, but their worrying doesn't help me deal with my own." Cassie nudged Leigh: "I know Hank's parents are just as concerned, but they're not Leigh's in-laws—not yet anyway, and she's not living downstairs with Mom and Dad's 'golden boy.'"

"What about your parents? Are they okay with your marriage?" Lindy inquired.

"Oh, they've been understanding and helpful, and we're not far from them. They seem to appreciate the Thompsons' giving us a place to stay, since they only have my old bedroom. They'd welcome me back home when Les leaves, but I can't do that, as easy as it might be. I'd feel like a child again, and now I must be the wife Les needs and wants. I hope to share a place with other wives near the base where he's assigned, at least until he ships out."

Ideas were forming in Leigh's relaxed mind, opened to the exchange of information between Lindy and Cassie. She did some mental figuring, then offered: "Cass, I don't know how long you'll want to stay near the base. But, you know, I'll graduate in less than a year now. If I get a job then and you have your spousal support—and maybe a job yourself, we could share an apartment, somewhere near the bus line. That way, if Les is able to come home on leave,

I can visit my family for a few days, and you and Les can have a place to yourselves. When Les is away, you wouldn't have to be *by* yourself—but you could just *be* yourself. We could be company for each other at times or have privacy when we want it. Parents would be only a bus ride away, but not worrisome.

"Oh, Leigh, that would be nice, wouldn't it?" Then, she added, with a wink at Lindy, "And, if by then you and Hank are married, when he's on leave, I'd be happy to go home to visit Mom and Dad and let you have the place to yourselves."

Lindy laughed: "Well, that only seems fair! Or, you know, you'd both always be welcome to visit us river folk, who just might be Leigh's in-laws."

"Thanks, I'll keep that in mind," Cassie giggled.

Leigh could only smile in response. The realization had come like a sudden rap on the head—she knew…She *knew*—these people, Hank's family, this river, Cassie and Les were her future. They would be part of her life, shape her life—and she would be part of their lives, until, one by one, they disappeared or faded away, leaving only aching hearts and memories. The clarity of the awareness was startling, yet, somehow, comforting. She settled back in the rocker, closed her eyes to the revelation, and relished the peace and stillness in her soul.

Chapter 38

Les carried the gear onto the skiff and took his place in front of the outboard motor. He waited while Hank untied the rope and threw it into the boat, picked up a paddle, and pushed the skiff away from the bank. Tom and Byrd were still loading into the other boat, when Hank called to them: "Uncle Byrd, we'll go tie up at the mouth of Big Creek. We may do a little swimming in the Blue Hole before we fish in the cove down near Uncle John's."

Byrd answered, "We'll see you down there later then."

When he had turned the boat to face upstream, Hank directed, "Okay, Les, crank her up."

As the motor droned and they headed against the current, Hank thought there could be nothing finer or freer than being on the Tennessee, with the misty breeze blowing against his face and the skiff slapping the choppy water. There must be something in his nature, in his soul, that always made him feel whole and alive when he returned to the mountains, to the valley where his family had lived for centuries, and to the river that his father knew so well and, even now, sustained their family. He knew he would carry this feeling, this soulful longing for place and people, wherever in the world his body might be found in the months and years ahead.

Les slowed the outboard, idled toward shore in a secluded inlet shaded by trees, then killed the motor. Hank, rope in hand, jumped to the rocky riverside, grabbing a crooked, overhanging tree trunk to pull himself up to the bank. "The gear will be safe here," he said, as he pulled the boat rope and tied it to the tree. "It's only about a half mile up the creek to the Blue Hole."

They trudged across the field and scaled the hill to the mountain road, from which a winding path led down to the icy chilled waters of the Blue Hole. Les declared: "It's beautiful here. Maybe, if and when you and Leigh get married, we can bring the girls up here, maybe even camp out sometimes. They'd love it."

"Well, I'm sure Uncle Byrd would let you and Cassie use his boat, if you want to do that anytime soon. The fellow that owns this property is a family friend. He'd give his permission for a campout on the river."

"That would be great. Cassie's pretty tough and outdoorsy. I think she'd like roughing it some." Les laughed: "You probably don't even know about your city gal. Think she'd like camping?"

Hank laughed: "I can't picture it, but I guess I'll just have to see. She might surprise both of us."

They began their descent to the creek—a narrow, rutted, rock-strewn way, here and there littered with broken branches. The path terminated at a series of rocks leading across the stream to a massive boulder, around which the downstream flow broke into two gurgling arms, before cascading over a gentle crest of rock into the Blue Hole.

The boys shed their shoes and clothes to their underwear and hanged their shirts and jeans on tree limbs before entering the icy water. "Oh, man, is this water cold!" Les exclaimed. "Think I'd be better off just taking a plunge and getting the shock behind me!"

"Wow, that's even colder than I remembered!" agreed Hank. "Think I'll go around to the hole and dive in—just go for it." He withdrew to the side of the creek and made his way down to the lower level of the hole.

A tree had fallen across the creek in front of the boulder and extended downstream into the Blue Hole. "I think I'll just walk this log down to the hole," Les said, as he stepped onto it and his toes gripped the bark. Les was almost to the deeper water, when the log rolled just enough to throw him off, sending him against the rocks, as he shouted, "Hank!"

Hank turned to see Les strike his head and descend into the darkness of the Blue Hole. Hank waited, expecting Les to come to the surface. When passing seconds told him something was wrong, Hank dived into the hole and swam toward his friend. Hank didn't know the depth of the water or what might be keeping Les under, but he knew he would find him—he would give his own life to find him, if need be.

After a minute or two, Hank's lungs were aching, and he surfaced to catch a breath before going under again. *There—he felt hair!* Hank reached his friend's shoulders, then under his arms, and pulled with every muscle in his body to bring Les to the surface. Something working against Hank's every effort refused to release Les from its grasp. Hank surfaced for a quick breath before diving down farther. He felt Les' leg, then his foot, twisted behind a section of fallen log. With his remaining strength, Hank forced the wood away and brought Les to the surface. Dragging him to the bank, Hank pulled Les onto the ground and began pumping his chest to expel water from his lungs. Each press on his friend's chest came with the prayer, *Please, God, let him live*. When at last Les coughed and spewed up what seemed a big drink of the creek, Hank, exhausted, fell on his back next to him.

After a few minutes, Les cleared his throat and gasped, "Thanks, buddy. I owe you." Les felt the back of his head, "Whew!"

Regaining his breath and shaking water from his ear, Hank asked, "What happened to you, man?"

"The log rolled, and I hit my head on the rocks. Guess I was knocked out. When I slid down into the hole, my foot must have caught between the rocks or something, and I was too out of it to get loose."

The friends lay there on the creek side for several minutes, before Hank said, "Don't know about you, but right now, some quiet fishing down at Uncle John's sounds good."

"I'm with you," Les agreed. "Just let me see if I can get up and walk straight with this pounding head."

"We can go on back to the house if you want to," Hank suggested.

"Oh, no," Les countered. "I've taken a couple of knock-out head blows before. Thankfully, it was just one rock banging against another," he chuckled. "I'll have a lump and a bruise, but I'll be okay."

As they retrieved their clothes and began to redress, Les put his hand on Hank's shoulder. "Really, thanks, Hank. You saved me. I really owe you."

Hank said, "Forget it, Les. You would have done the same for me." Hank gave Les a fake punch to the gut, "If I had been the one busting it and nearly drowning before even beginning to swim."

The boys returned to the waiting skiff. In short order, Hank had the motor humming gently, while the current helped propel them back downstream to the fishing spot near Uncle John's field. Hank thought about the fragility of life—how, in a moment, circumstances can change the course of one's future, perhaps forevermore. He silently thanked God that his friend was sitting in front of him, perhaps bumped and bruised, but ready to return to life with his wife, who loved him and waited for his return from the river or from wherever that life might take him.

Chapter 39
June 15, 1942

Eliza knocked on the frame of Hank's bedroom door, opened to the sound of Glenn Miller's orchestra emanating from Nancy's radio in her bedroom across the hall. *"Moonlight Serenade,"* Hank thought as he looked at the picture in his wallet, *will always remind me of Leigh and the way her hair reflects light, like gold or silk.* Eliza knocked again. "Oh, hey, Mom, I'm just about ready."

"Have you double-checked your bag—underwear, socks, change of clothes, papers, ID?" Eliza quizzed.

"Think it's all there. I think they'll send most of it back to you after they issue all the GI garb and supplies."

"I'll make sure everything is clean, neat, organized, and ready for you when you come home."

Eliza made a hasty retreat across the hall to Nancy's room, where she knew she could shed tears openly with her daughter. She wanted to present a stalwart, confident demeanor before her son, but the bold, courageous girl she once had been was now "Mother." The demands of the role in this time of war were almost more than she could bear. Already women just like her were receiving reports of sons injured or killed in battle or missing. Younger wives, like Cassie, were sending their husbands off without promise of any tomorrows, and some were receiving them back in flag-draped coffins. And those with children who might never know their fathers—*oh, how sad and fearful to think about bringing up fatherless children!*

Nancy had just finished tying a blue ribbon around her head to hold back her curls when her mother entered the room, closed the door, and sat on Nancy's bed. The handkerchief Eliza held over her mouth to muffle her sobs was soaked with an abundance of tears. Nancy moved to sit at her mother's side, putting her arm around Eliza's shoulders and drawing her close. Nancy thought, *I feel completely dried up—no tears left.* First there were tears for Jeff and the realization of her loss before she had even fully recognized his significance in her life. Then, last night she had wept herself to sleep in the knowledge that Hank would be lost to her for months, if not years, and perhaps, even forever. The thought of so many families experiencing the same penetrating pain of fearful emotions gave no comfort or consolation. This misery was unique to every individual, who, for love of country, would be called upon to "Stay busy," as her mother had said—stay busy with the war effort, stay busy with conservation and rationing, stay busy just trying to hold oneself together to face whatever challenges would have to be met, whatever mountains would have to be scaled. And the ultimate question: What's on the other side of that mountain—a peaceful valley, or just another mountain?

Josh Hodge pulled the Tudor around to the front of the house and waited while Eliza and Nancy said their goodbyes to Hank. Only a few miles away, the same scene was playing at the Thompson home. In just minutes, Josh and Hank would pick up Les, his parents' precious only child and son. But Cassie would be the protagonist there, the young wife who, in just the last couple of days, had learned she would be mother to a child whose father might be to him— or her, only a grainy black and white photo in the family album.

I was there when he was born, Josh thought, *perfect, whole. Now, I am sending him off into this merciless war—even made it possible*. Josh knew, though, it was just a matter of time. If he had not signed the papers for Hank's enlistment, Hank would have forged ahead on his own, as soon as he had reached eighteen. Josh's only consolation was that his son was healthy, strong, intelligent, and, above all, lived by a strong faith that Josh prayed would not be shaken, no matter how fierce the battle, how grue-some the consequences—or how final the temporal conflict. *I want to see Morgan. I need to see Morgan.* Josh determined he, Eliza, and Nancy would take some time off as soon as possible for a train trip to Cincinnati to see their friend and spiritual mentor and his wife, Madeline. *Morgan has faced this and en-dured the worst somehow—with hope and optimism.* Josh had the answers in his head, but he struggled to apply them to his aching heart. *I've got to see beyond all this.* He remembered Hank's words: *"We talk about having faith, but the time comes when we have to prove it."*

Josh and Hank turned into the Thompsons' driveway. On the porch were Francine and Lester, supporting his wife as she brushed tears from her face and they watched Les and Cassie on the side-walk, sharing parting words and a final kiss. Cassie's red eyes and swollen face made apparent their last moments together had been bittersweet.

Les released his wife from their embrace, he picked up his bag, and walked to the waiting car. "Les!" He heard Cassie's cry and turned, dropping the bag and receiving his rushing wife into his arms for one more kiss. He kissed each of her hands he removed from his neck. "I have to go, Cass. You know I love you. I trust you to take good care of yourself and our little Lester the Third or Lessie," he tried to say with a smile. "I'll be back. Take care of Mom and Dad and spend some time with Leigh. She'll need you too."

"I will," she whispered. "I love you."

Hank turned to enter the back seat of the Hodges' sedan and closed the door. Hank noticed the shirt Les was wearing was wet where tears had been spilled by Cassie, by his mother, perhaps, by Les, Sr.

Chapter 40

Vehicles filled the lot at "Fort O," as Camp Oglethorpe was called, and civilians mingled here and there for word of whether their loved ones had passed the final physical and would be leaving on the buses, waiting in line nearby to transport new soldiers to their designated locations. Josh waited in the sparse shade of one of the few available trees near the induction center. He had brought a thermos of cold water, from which he sipped occasionally, and once had wet his handkerchief to wipe his face, not so much from the heat, as from the burning sting of nerves and anxiety that threatened his heart. *I have to survive this*, he told himself. *I have to be around for Hank— and Nancy. Even she will be leaving sometime. I might lose them both.*

An hour passed. The next hour had begun. Josh noticed men beginning to leave from the side door of the building to line up at the waiting buses. Each would scan the throng of families and friends until he spotted the one, or ones, to whom he would wave, blow a kiss, or give a salute. Then, these loved ones would move as close as possible to the buses, just to maintain some contact with their soldier—just another smile, another silent "I love you" blown into the air, another glimpse of precious life and connection.

Then, a young man exited the main doors of the center. Head down, his eyes only glanced right, then left, seemingly anticipating the approach of one he knew. Josh watched as an older version of the young man came from behind and placed a hand on the son's shoulder. The son turned and collapsed against his father and cried unabashedly. The father grasped him firm against his chest. Josh was reminded of how Hank, as a small child, would fall asleep on his father's chest, and Josh had to resist the urge just to squeeze Hank into himself—he loved him so much.

Josh walked across the sidewalk to a place where he could see the men forming the bus lines. *Wait...there's Les...where's Hank?* He noticed Les, frowning, looking in his direction.

"Dad," Josh heard next to him. Turning, Josh saw his son, dejected, miserable.

In response to his father's questioning expression, Hank could only say, "4-F, Dad. I'm 4-F."

As soon as the words passed his lips, Les crashed into Hank. He had broken the bus line to come to his friend and almost lifted Hank from his feet with a bear hug. "Hank, I'm so sorry. It's all my fault. I'm so sorry."

Hank shook his head. "Nobody's fault. Just something that happened."

"Forgive me. I love you, Bud," Les pleaded.

"Les, there's nothing to forgive. Maybe this was meant to be. I'll be okay. It just hurts right now." Hank continued: "Just remember, I'll be doing whatever I can to support you back here, and I'll take care of Cassie and the baby while you're gone."

"Thanks, Hank. I'll write and, hopefully, see you again." Turning to shake Josh's hand, Les added, "Goodbye, Mr. Hodge. Thanks for everything."

Still bewildered, Josh replied, "You're welcome, son. Take care. We'll be praying for you." As Les ran back to the bus line, Josh added, "God bless you, Les!" Les looked back and waved just as his line mounted the steps to the bus that would take them to Fort Benning, Georgia, where they would join the Second Armored Division.

Josh and Hank rode in silence for a time. Hank leaned his head against the car window. Josh glimpsed tears streaming down Hank's cheek, and he sensed his son was struggling to maintain his composure. Though Hank was brokenhearted and would need his father's comfort and support, Josh had to say a silent prayer of thanks that Hank was not on one of those buses. "4-F" was a terrible blow to a man, sometimes a stigma and source of discrimination and ridicule. But it wasn't life-threatening, and a man who knew his true worth could prove his character and make important contributions without risking being blown to bits. Josh reminded himself to keep such thoughts to himself, to be patient, and to ease into communication. "Do you want to talk, son."

"Not much to say," was Hank's dispirited reply.

"Do you feel like telling me what happened? Why did Les say it was all his fault?" Josh asked, not knowing whether or not he would get an answer.

After a few seconds, Hank sighed, wiped his cheek with the back of his hand, and explained: "We didn't tell anyone, but Les hit his head at the Blue Hole and knocked himself out before sliding into the water. When he sank, he must have got his foot stuck in the rocks. When he didn't come up, I went down after him—a couple of times." Hank paused and let out a deep, cleansing breath. "My ear drum's perforated. Must have happened then—the only thing I can figure. I knew my ear was stopped up and a little achy. Just figured I still had water in it. The doc said the eardrum's perforated—automatic disqualification."

"I'm sorry, son. Will it heal?" Josh inquired.

"I don't know, maybe, maybe not." Hank hesitated, then said, "Seems at least for now I've lost a good bit of hearing in that ear."

Josh hesitated, then offered: "I know you haven't had time to think about an alternate plan. But if you want to go on to college, we'll help as we can."

"I don't know. I'll think about it. Maybe I'll just get a job somewhere where I can at least help the war effort—do something that makes me feel I'm supporting Les.

They rode again in silence, then Josh said, "I can only imagine how bad you feel, but Les is likely feeling just as bad, believing his accident ruined your plans."

Hank responded, "Well, I hope he'll get over that and maybe be glad I'm around here to see about Cassie and the baby." Hank straightened up in the seat and exhaled. "You know, Dad, whatever the future holds, it's going to take a lot of courage and strength to be labeled '4-F' and still be considered a man. Not to take anything away from Les and those in the fray, but it's easy for people to see you as a man, when you're wearing the uniform and carrying a weapon. It'll be a lot harder for me to prove."

As Josh drove the car in one of the narrow lanes crossing the bridge to the north side, he struggled to restrain his own tears. He was touched by the wisdom and maturity revealed by Hank's words. He paused for control, then declared, "Son, today I see you as one of the best men I've ever known, in uniform or out. I believe you have a fine future ahead of you."

"Thanks," Hank said. Stopping at the light on Frazier, Josh looked at his son, who added, "I love you, Dad."

Josh replied, "I love you, too, Hank. Never forget that."

Josh pulled the car into the garage and turned off the engine. "You want to go on inside and tell your mom and Nancy, or you want me to be with you."

Hank waited, then answered. "No, you do what you need to do down here. I'll tell them. I know they'll be relieved, and they won't understand … well, how it is. But my '4-F' future begins today."

Josh said, "Yes, but you're man enough to handle it. That's a fact."

Hank took his bag and made a long, slow climb up the basement stairs to the kitchen.

Chapter 41

Eliza was seated in the living room, elbows propped on her desk, her forehead in her hands, undisturbed by Hank's entrance from the garage. Hank stood in the kitchen doorway and watched her for a moment before speaking. *She still looks young and so beautiful*, he thought, *likely praying*. He knew this day had been hard on his parents and sister. *Well, the first positive in all this is easing their anxiety.*

"Mom," Hank interrupted Eliza, and she turned in disbelief toward his voice.

"Hank? Oh, Hank!" Eliza jumped up to enfold him in her arms. Hank wondered, *How did I not realize she is so much smaller than I am?* He could rest his chin on his mother's head, and her form seemed too slight for the woman he knew to be so strong, not only physically, but in spirit and will. "What happened? Why are you back?" she asked, stroking his face and cupping it in her hand.

"Disqualified, Mom—'4-F,'" he stated.

"Oh, Hank, I'm sorry. I know you are disappointed. But I must admit I'm relieved. I've been praying for your safety and for Les, but never did I expect to see you there in the doorway." Eliza pulled him toward the divan. "Come, sit. Tell me what happened."

Hank recounted events as he had for his father, after which Eliza stated, "Well, I thought you seemed distracted and not responsive at times lately, but it may have just been a problem with your hearing."

"Maybe so." Hank stood and walked to the living room window that faced the sloping green lawn that gave his father so much pleasure. *Green from all the sweat of mowing*, Hank smiled as he thought. "Mom, I'm going to call Leigh. I need to tell her what's happened. Then, I think I'll go down and see if Dad minds my using the car to drive over to her house. See how she really feels about having a '4-F' boyfriend."

"Oh, Hank, she would not be the girl for you, if she's so shallow that would make any difference. If you like, invite her over here for dinner," Eliza offered.

"Thanks, Mom. I'll ask her." Hank picked up his bag to take to his bedroom. "Is Nut Jar upstairs?"

"No, she's visiting Jeff's mother. She'll be back in time for dinner."

Eliza was washing vegetables at the kitchen sink when Hank returned and opened the door to the garage stairway. He paused to look again at Eliza. "Mom." When he got her attention, he continued, "I love you, Mom."

Eliza shook her head, "I know, dear—and, oh, how I love you, too."

In a moment, time and life began whirling like a funnel cloud, as Hank burst through the kitchen door to the garage and yelled, "Mom, it's Dad! Call an ambulance! Call an ambulance!"

Without question, Eliza raced to the phone and called the operator to request emergency service. Then, she followed Hank back down to the garage. "Hank, where are you?"

"Over here, Mom! He's fallen over here on the other side of the car."

Eliza hurried around the back of the car to find Hank holding his father's head in his lap. Josh was pale and barely breathing. Eliza fell to her knees beside him, held his hand, and begged, "Josh, oh, Josh, Josh, don't leave me."

"Mom, what about the ambulance?" Hank asked, but Eliza seemed not to hear. "Mom! Listen! Did you call the ambulance?"

Hank had never seen his mother so frightened, as she looked at him and answered, "Yes, Hank, I did. I gave them our address. They said they're less than five minutes way."

Hank knew his mother was praying as fervently as he was, when they heard the sound of the siren. The ambulance pulled into the driveway, stopping outside the open garage door. The siren went silent, but lights continued to flash, as three men rushed in, one carrying a stretcher, another a case, and the doctor ordering, "Stand back, please, stand back!" Hank held his mother as the man took Josh's pulse and listened to his heart. The medic picked up a pill bottle that had rolled behind the car's tire. Hank hadn't noticed it or the tiny pills scattered nearby. Glancing at the label, the doctor barked to the others, "Transport immediately!"

While Josh was placed on the stretcher and loaded into the waiting vehicle, the medic explained to Eliza: "He's had an apparent heart attack. We're taking him to Newell Hospital. We'll try to stabilize him as soon as we get him there. You can follow as soon as you like, but it may be a while before you can see him. Are you and your son the immediate family?"

Eliza hesitated, stuttering, "Uh, n-no, no …"

Hank said, "My sister's not at home. I'll call her. We'll pick her up and be there directly."

"Good. Just come in the emergency entrance and check in at the desk."

Hank helped Eliza up the steps to the kitchen and seated her at the table. "I'll call Mrs. Langston, tell Nancy what's happened and that we're picking her up. Is the number in your book in the phone stand?"

Eliza was motionless and quiet.

"Mom! Do you have Mrs. Langston's phone number?"

Eliza mumbled, "What? Oh, yes, dear. In the book."

Hank hurried to the stand, found the book, scanned a few pages before finding "Ethel Langston, Jeff's mother" and began dialing her phone number. Each return of the dial seemed to consume precious time. *Has this always been so slow?!* When Mrs. Langston answered, Hank said, "Mrs. Langston, this is Nancy's brother, Hank. May I speak with her? It's urgent." He tried to be patient and calm while waiting to hear his sister's voice.

"Hank, where are you? I thought you'd be on your way…"

Hank interrupted, "Sis, I'll tell you later. Right now, Dad is very ill, and he's on his way to the hospital. Mom and I are coming by to pick you up. Be ready." Hank dropped the receiver back into its cradle. He went to his parents' bedroom, found his mother's purse on the dresser, and took a sweater for her from the shelf in the closet.

Returning to the kitchen, he took the spare set of keys from the cupboard and handed the purse and sweater to Eliza, while he asked, "Mom, is there anything else you need?"

"No, no, son." Eliza was so compliant, Hank feared for her well-being. This was not the mother he thought he knew—but then, this was the wife fearful of losing the one person she loved above all others in this world.

Nancy was waiting on Ethel Langston's porch when the Hodges' sedan pulled up to the curb. Nancy gave Jeff's mother a quick hug and "Thank you," before racing down the steps, opening the car door, and sliding into the back seat. "What is it, Hank? What's happened?"

Again, Hank tried to remain calm for the sake of his mother and sister. "The ambulance medic said Dad has had an apparent heart attack. The doctors will try to stabilize him. It may take a while, but we can see him as soon as possible."

Nancy tried to digest the information, then remembered: "Hank, why are you here? I thought you were supposed to leave today."

"Well, it seems I couldn't pass the physical—perforated eardrum."

Nancy only responded, "I'm sorry."

Hank continued: "That doesn't seem that important right now. I'm thankful I can be here—with you and Mom."

Nancy placed her hand on Eliza's shoulder. "Mother, are you all right?"

Eliza waited to answer, then said softly, "No, dear, I'm not. I won't be all right until I know your father is."

Nancy reclined against the cushioned seat back and watched, without seeing, the passing buildings. She felt herself functioning on nothing but sheer emotion and adrenaline. All she could do was pray. Perhaps, someday, she could do more—if not for her father, for others like him. Pray and stay busy, her mother had said—*Pray and stay busy.*

The hospital emergency room was unexpectedly quiet, only two nurses—one behind the reception desk and one standing at the end of the counter charting records. Hank addressed the one behind the desk: "We are the Hodge family. My father was just brought in by ambulance."

"Oh, yes, Mr. Hodge," she replied. Waving a hand at the nearby assemblage of chairs, she added: "If you will just take a seat in the waiting area, I'll let the doctor know you've arrived."

"Thank you," Hank responded. "Come on, Mother. Let's sit over here." His hand under Eliza's arm, Hank guided her to a seat, and he and Nancy flanked her in adjacent chairs. For nearly twenty minutes, they sat in silence, nothing more they could say or do, except lay silent petitions before the Giver of life and Receiver of souls.

"Mrs. Hodge?" Before them stood a doctor who introduced himself as Dr. Castleberry, "Josh's cardiologist, his heart doctor. I happened to be on call when Josh was brought in."

They were all perplexed by his words, but Hank spoke up: "Cardiologist? We had no idea there was anything wrong with his heart?"

"Well, yes, he has seen me a few times in the last several months. He's a good man who loves his family. I'm sure he didn't want to worry you."

Nancy asked, "Is he going to be all right?"

"Truthfully, his heart is very weak. He is on oxygen, and we gave him some IV medication. Perhaps, with some rest, he will pull through this, but I can make no promises. It's a very delicate situation."

Nancy put her head in her hand to shield her tears. Eliza remained quiet and fixed on the doctor's face, until she uttered the words, "I must see him."

"I think that would be advisable, but, please, try not to upset him." Addressing Hank and Nancy, he continued, "Give your mother about five minutes, then, you can visit him briefly—and calmly, or, please, leave the room." Taking Eliza's hand, the doctor asked, "May I assist you, Mrs. Hodge?"

Jan Dearman

Through timeless fog Eliza moved—a stranger in a strange world of emotions so intense and devastating, even now, they might have vanquished what was once her indomitable spirit and will. The room where Josh lay was quiet. A nurse, without words, hovered around the bed with tender ministrations, then, with a sympathetic nod toward Eliza, glided from the room. Eliza went to Josh's bedside and took his hand—tanned, rugged, the tufts of hair on his fingers now gray, his wedding band narrower, but shiny smooth from years of wear.

"Eliza." Josh whispered, struggling to open his eyes.

Eliza forced herself to think through the fog and to speak without crumbling. "Yes, dear. I'm here. I love you, dear."

"Eliza, love you." He closed his eyes while speaking, "Hank…come home?…Nancy?"

"Yes, Josh, Hank came home. He and Nancy are waiting outside to see you." Silent tears streaked her cheeks, as she squeezed Josh's hand. Perhaps he wouldn't slip away if her grasp was tight enough.

A soft rap on the door was followed by "Mother, is it all right to come in?"

"Yes, Hank." Eliza said, "Josh, the children are here to see you." Still holding his hand, Eliza moved down the bedside, allowing Hank and Nancy to come near his side.

Josh's eyes opened again, "Son...home."

"Yes, Dad, I'm home—not going away."

Josh seemed to smile. "Good," he whispered, closing his eyes. Then, he looked at his daughter. "Nancy...safe."

Nancy choked, "Yes, Dad, I'm safe. I love you."

"Love you," Josh seemed to speak with increased strength. "Love you, son."

Hank answered, "I love you, Dad."

"Hank!" Josh blurted a whisper.

"Yes, Dad?"

"Take care...mother...Nancy."

Josh's hand seemed to tighten around Eliza's fingers. She said, "Josh, you need to rest. We want to take you home. No more words."

Seeing the unseen, Josh whispered, "Yes. Rest...home...Morgan," and his fingers released Eliza's hand.

Chapter 42

Hank paced the platform, as he waited for the train from Cincinnati to arrive. He realized the smell of the station would always induce memories of his father's death. The hustle and bustle of activity—passengers scurrying, baggage moving, soldiers coming and going, the tears of loved ones marking both arrivals and departures—all of it seemed a fitting analogy for the circumstances in which he now found himself, as he took the lead in planning and preparing for the funeral. He followed his mother's limited advice and direction—she still was too distraught to tackle much. And Hank loved and appreciated his sister more than ever. Nancy was a tremendous help—supporting Eliza, preparing for their house guests, greeting the brethren and friends as they brought food, and keeping a record of their generosity for future "Thank-you" notes. As his father would have wanted and expected, Hank was trying to stay clear-headed and focused to get things done—first and foremost, to see to Aunt Maddie and Uncle Morgan's arrival and comfort. How thankful he was that, though arthritis had slowed them both, they were healthy and fit enough to make the trip.

Hank noted the time on the station clock and heard the horn as the train growled into the terminal, almost on the dot of the scheduled arrival time. The train doors opened, and pullmen exited to position steps for the safe egress of the passengers. Walking from car to car, Hank looked for the Kendalls, until he was nearly to the end of the train. Thinking they might have passed him and were waiting in the station, he turned to retrace his steps, only to hear a booming voice shout, "John Henry Hodge!"

Hank whirled around to see the comforting sight of Uncle Morgan and Aunt Maddie, trudging alongside the cars as they labored under the weight of their luggage. Setting their bags down, they stopped on the walkway to greet Hank, and Morgan received him into his outstretched arms, as he continued, "If you aren't the spittin' image of Josh Hodge!" The dam of will power holding back Hank's tears burst upon Morgan's broad chest, as Madeline caressed and rubbed the boy's back and murmured, "Sweet, sweet child."

"There, there, son," soothed Morgan, "tears are a blessing from God to soothe a hurting heart. I dare say you haven't shed enough of them since your Daddy passed."

When Hank regained his bearing, he took a handkerchief from his jacket pocket and wiped his eyes and nose. "Thank you, Uncle Morgan…Aunt Maddie…for coming. Just knowing you would be here has helped us the last couple of days."

"Son, I loved your Daddy like a brother—and we are brothers in the Lord. I would be here regardless, but I am honored to speak the eulogy."

"Let me get these bags for you." Hank picked up the two large bags, and Morgan and Madeline each took a train case. "I can tuck those small bags under each arm," Hank offered.

"No, no, son, we can manage them." Morgan smiled, "We're south of the Mason-Dixon now. You'll get this poor old black man in trouble, if they see me loading you down with baggage."

As they made a slow approach to the terminal, Hank said, "Uncle Morgan, the last word Dad uttered before passing was your name—he said, "Rest...home...Morgan."

"Well, Hank, your Dad is now resting peacefully in that home beyond time, and he was letting me know not to dilly-dally in meeting him there."

Hank parked the sedan at the end of the walk. He opened the front car door for Morgan and the rear door for Madeline, with the words, "Just leave your bags, and I'll bring them in later." There were only three steps to the front porch, and Hank surmised the train trip already had been challenging for the elderly couple, considering the lack of space and amenities in the segregated cars. Morgan used the porch railing to steady himself as he went up to the front door, and

Hank held Madeline's hand and put his arm around her waist for support, as they followed behind him.

Nancy opened the door before Morgan reached it. "Uncle Morgan, it's so good to see you!" Nancy's arms encircled his expansive middle, and she leaned her head against his chest. "Thank you for making the trip. Please, come in and rest. Mother's in the den," she stated, motioning him toward the room behind her. Giving Madeline a hug, Nancy added: "And Aunt Maddie, please, come in and make yourself at home. You must be exhausted."

"Thank you, child. Yes, we're both a little weary." Madeline removed her hat and placed it on her purse in the chair near the phone nook in the front hall. "I'll go back and see Eliza—sit with her for a while."

Eliza was resting on the sofa in front of the fireplace. Seeing her guests arrive, she said simply, "Morgan, Madeline, God bless you." Morgan sat on the couch next to Eliza, taking her hand and hiding it within both of his. Madeline sat on her other side and placed her gloved hand on Eliza's arm.

When they were settled, Nancy asked, "Can I get you something to drink? And we have all kinds of food in the kitchen and dining room if you're hungry. I can fix you a plate, or there are plates on the table if you want to choose for yourself."

Morgan answered, "If you've got some tea or coffee on hand, I wouldn't mind some of either. How about you, Maddie?"

"Yes, thanks, Nancy, that would be welcomed," she answered. "We can see to ourselves in a bit as far as food is concerned. I know we're both hungry. We only took a few snacks on the train, and it was a long ride."

Hank entered the den to inform them, "Uncle Morgan and Aunt Maddie, your bags are in mother and … uh, the downstairs bedroom."

Turning to Eliza, Maddie declared, "Eliza, we don't want to run you out of your room."

Eliza's smile was sad, sweet, as she replied, "No, Maddie, please, we've planned it. It's freshly made up, it has a shower room, we've made space for your things, and you won't have to climb stairs. Besides, though some of Josh's belongings are still there, he isn't. I'll be taking him with me upstairs, downstairs—wherever I go, he'll be with me."

Morgan squeezed Eliza's hand and said, "Thank you, Eliza. Your hospitality is much appreciated."

Eliza responded, "Morgan, you and Maddie have always opened your home to us, so graciously and freely. And it's such a comfort to have you here."

"Rejoice with them that do rejoice, and weep with them that weep," Morgan quoted the familiar

Scripture. "We've done a lot of rejoicing over the years. Now comes the time for weeping. One binds us in friendship and joy—the other, in brotherhood and love."

Hank was pleased to see his mother communicating with the Kendalls—the most she had spoken since the death. He waited for a pause in their conversation and asked, "Mother, would you mind my going to see Leigh. I haven't seen her since the night before I was supposed to leave?"

"No, Hank, please, go. I've got Morgan and Madeline here now. You need a break."

"Thanks, Mom." Hank gave his mother a kiss on the cheek, and said to their guests, "Hope you'll excuse me, Aunt Maddie, Uncle Morgan. If I'm not back by the time you turn in, thanks again for coming. Love you both."

"You too, son. Tell your best girl we look forward to meeting her. We hear she may be a keeper," Morgan smiled.

"Yes, sir, right now that's my plan," Hank replied, stopping at the phone nook to call Leigh to let her know he would "be there in fifteen."

Chapter 43

Leigh placed the phone back in its cradle. Charles was sitting in the living room, smoking his pipe and reading the daily war report in the newspaper, when Leigh approached him. "Dad, Hank is coming by. He wants to talk with me. Do you mind?"

"Well, what can I say? He's already on his way," came his curt reply. A pause, then Charles dropped the paper on his lap and looked at Leigh with apology, "Leigh, I'm sorry. Slipping back into my old ways. Guess I'm still a work in progress. I don't mind Hank's coming over."

Leigh dared further conversation with Charles: "Dad, Hank's going through a bad time right now. The same day he failed his induction physical, his dad had a heart attack and died. He and his dad were really close. Hank needs his friends right now."

Charles remembered his feeling of dark emptiness when he lost Roger and how he needed to reach out to Rose and Leigh and Alice. "I understand. I'll take my pipe and paper back to the kitchen. You and Hank can talk up here in the living room. I might even try to interest your mother in a game of Canasta. She's probably playing her nightly Solitaire on the kitchen table right now." Charles held his pipe between his teeth, as he rose, collected his paper, and straightened the items on his chairside table. As he passed by Leigh on his way to the kitchen, she touched his arm and said, "Thank you."

Charles placed his hand on Leigh's and said, "Remember—a work in progress. Please be patient with this bitter old Yankee geezer."

Leigh led Hank into the living room, where they sat on the couch, close enough to be friendly, but not so close as to be unmindful of the gravity of the circumstances about which they would speak.

Leigh asked, "Hank, is there anything we can do? I know this is a terrible time for you and your family."

Hank leaned forward, arms on his knees, studying his clenched hands. Leigh knew he was trying to control his emotion, when he answered, "Thanks, I don't think so. I would like for you to come to the funeral Friday—your family too if they want to. It's at 10 o'clock at the church building. Morgan Kendall—we call him "Uncle Morgan"— has come in from Cincinnati to do the eulogy. I'd like for you to meet him. He and his wife, Madeline, are wonderful people. And, of course, afterward, there'll be enough food to feed the Army." Hank looked up at her: "Of course, I won't really know about Army food."

Leigh laid her hand on his arm. "Hank, when you called to tell me about the physical at the induction station—and then about the accident on the river, I was shocked. You and Les never let on that anything had happened." She admitted, "Of course, there was no need to upset Cassie."

"No, we thought it could be just put behind us and forgotten," Hank agreed. "And maybe we can forget someday," he sighed. "Les feels kind of guilty—thinks it was his fault I was rejected. You know how people tend to think about '4-Fs.'" He looked at Leigh: "How do you feel about '4-Fs'?"

"Why? How am I supposed to feel? All I've felt is a little sad you didn't get to do what you wanted and to be with Les. I'm sorry about your ear problem. But, beyond that, what's changed? You're still the same Hank. Truthfully, I'm overjoyed you can be here, and our future's more secure than if you were someplace getting shot at!" Leigh took Hank's hand. "And, right now, all I feel is such sadness that you are going through this loss. I know how close you and your father were. And I know he would be proud of the man you are. No silly '4-F' tag can change that."

Hank wiped a tear from his cheek and said, "Thanks, Leigh. I needed to hear that. You know...I love you."

"Yes, and I love you too. Hopefully, we can outgrow and outlive all this sadness and all this turmoil that's made this whole world one big ball of mess!"

Hank realized he had not smiled for a long time, until he felt himself smiling at Leigh. "I want to be able to tackle the mess with you by my side."

Leigh said, "I want that too."

Hank sighed again, "Well, I've got to get back to the family." He went to the door. "When everything has settled—the funeral, going through Dad's belongings, anything else Mom needs me to do, I'm going to look for a job. I want to support the war effort somehow. Maybe later on, I'll go to college, but that doesn't seem important right now."

"I'll see you at the funeral," Leigh told him, before advising: "You take all the time you need in the next few weeks. I'm not going anywhere. I'll be here when you have more time and feel like talking or doing something. I'm trying to spend more time with Cassie these days. She's missing Les something awful. And, on top of that, her morning sickness has been pretty rough."

Hank asked, "Is everything okay with the baby?"

"Everything seems to be fine. I think they expect the baby to be born maybe in January, February, I'm not sure."

Hank opened the door, saying, "I'll see you Friday. Plan to stay after and eat with us, if you can—maybe bring Cassie, if she feels well enough." He turned back to give Leigh a kiss on the cheek and whisper, "Love you. Thanks."

"Thanks for what?" asked Leigh.

"For loving me," he stated, before closing the door behind him.

Leigh went into the kitchen, where she found Charles and Rose chatting, neat stacks of playing cards aligned before them.

"How is Hank holding up?" Rose asked.

Leigh took a glass from the cabinet, opened the refrigerator door, and retrieved a milk bottle. "He's really sad, but he's managing. I know he feels he has to be the man of the house, and Mrs. Hodge is relying on him right now."

"Didn't he graduate early so he could enlist?" asked Charles.

"Yes. He was rejected because of a perforated eardrum." Leigh took some crème wafers from the cookie jar. "They think he got it when Les slipped and knocked himself out and nearly drowned at the Blue Hole. Hank saved him. He dived down pretty deep to get him, and the pressure on his ear may have been just too much. That's all they can figure. But, whatever the cause, he's '4-F.'"

Charles seemed to be pondering the information, and Rose said, "That's a hard thing to bear for some young men."

Leigh answered, "Yes, but Hank's got a strong character. He's smart and level-headed. He'll be man enough not to be thwarted by some old label."

Charles asked, "What's he going to do?"

Leigh replied, "I think, once all his dad's affairs are settled, he'll get a job. He says he wants to support the war effort somehow—and I know, by that, he's thinking of Les in particular." Leigh returned the bottle to the fridge. "I think I'll go up and read for a while before turning in early—I'm kind of tired." She started toward the stairs.

"Leigh!" Charles' unexpected address startled her, and she pivoted toward him.

"Yes, sir?"

"When the time is right, tell Hank to come see me. I think I can make that job happen—something that definitely will support the war effort. It will take a smart, level-headed man."

Leigh moved to stand before Charles and asked in amazement, "You would do that for Hank?"

Charles took Leigh's hand. "I would do that for my daughter and the man she loves—assuming her assessment of him is accurate," he smiled.

Leigh sought for words, then said, "Thank you, Dad. I know Hank would never disappoint you." Leigh looked at her mother and saw a new smile—an open, honest, contented smile. *Just maybe*, she thought, *our little piece of the world is not such a mess after all*.

Chapter 44

Eliza sat before the cloth-covered cardboard casket that contained the shell of her beloved Josh. His earthly vessel deserved finer packaging, but conservation for the war effort impacted every aspect of life—and death. Morgan was making his introductory remarks. Eliza noted, though Morgan had slowed with age, his voice was as resonant and powerful as the day of her marriage—the deep, rich bass voice resounding from the rock under the mighty oak and echoing through the valley.

"Josh Hodge was a riverboat captain when I first met him—young, strong, smart, courageous—much like his son, John Henry—Hank, right here." Morgan motioned to Hank. "He was in love with rivers and boats, and he gave them all his time and attention—that is, until his path crossed the path of Eliza McNeal—that path being the Trail of Tears, on which this seemingly delicate little lady we see before us rode horseback, delivering mail from loaded saddle bags weighing nearly half as much she does. Theirs was a beautiful story of love, commitment, and marriage that lasted nearly thirty years and produced two fine children, Nancy Jewel and John Henry. Josh and Eliza were unselfish enough to share with me and my wife the joy of their children. I loved

Josh like a brother, and we have been to his children 'Uncle Morgan' and 'Aunt Maddie.' He was my co-worker, my friend, my brother in faith, and my support in time of sorrow, as I hope to be to his precious wife and children in this time of terrible sadness and loss.

"Those of us who know, beyond the bond of time, there is something far better awaiting the faithful, can have confidence—that 'far better' Josh has achieved. But for us who are left behind it's a hard thing to make our emotions accept what we know to be true in our heads. We are selfish creatures—we want to hold to our loved ones, keep them, cherish them, never let them leave. But, alas, it cannot be. Each of us is just a temporal package in a material world. Neither the package nor the world can endure. Only the precious soul within the package—the soul that looks beyond the wars, the bloodshed, the hatred and inhumanity of man toward man—the soul that endures to the end of the trail—that soul is victorious, that soul is immortal. My comfort in the loss of my friend, Josh Hodge, is that he has achieved victory, immortality, and perhaps, is telling my beloved son, Caleb, 'not much longer now—your daddy's right behind me.'"

Morgan took a handkerchief from his pocket and wiped his face. He looked down at the Book before him, then faced the assembly and began to quote the familiar Scripture: "The Lord is my Shepherd; I shall not want…"

Leigh noticed Cassie, next to her, paused from time to time the continual twisting of the handkerchief in her lap to dab her eyes. Leigh could only imagine the tumble of sad and frightening scenarios playing out in her friend's mind, exaggerated by the physical changes of pregnancy occurring in Cassie's still teenaged body. Leigh wondered where any of them would be when this conflict came to an end—if it did.

"…Yea, though I walk through the valley of the shadow of death…"

Leigh thought about the words Morgan spoke. Nearly the whole world was walking through the valley shadowed by the hovering darkness of death. But death's heavy cloud had burst and was threatening to inundate some, like the Hodges—not that they weren't aware the rains might come, but they were early rains. *What had Josh's preacher said that time in class about the early rain…it causes the seed to germinate?*

"Surely goodness and mercy shall follow me all the days of my life…"

Leigh thought it ironic how the heartache of death made her think about the hope of new life. In the upheaved world in which she and those who had gathered at the Diner found themselves, the heart-ache of death seemed to promise only more of the same.

Those closest to the Hodges followed the cas-ket to the gravesite. Leigh recognized Louise's hus-band, Tom, as one of the pallbearers. She assumed Hank's cousins, J. T., Thomas, and William were among them—she hadn't met them yet. There were Mr. Thompson, Les' father, and...*Coach Leonard—so thoughtful of him to be here for Hank!*

Morgan Kendall stood at the head of the cof-fin to give the benediction. Leigh thought she would never hear a voice so soul-penetrating as his, as it moved over the assemblage gathered around the Hodges. He spoke of the brevity and uncertainty of this life and of the beauty and security of the timeless existence promised the faithful. Morgan concluded the benediction by addressing the family: "Eliza, cherish the memories you have of your years with Josh. Nancy and Hank, cherish the memories of your father. Thank God, your greater Father, that He gave us the power to preserve these treasures in our hearts. All of you, family and friends who weep at the loss of Josh Hodge, cherish the blessing of tears, a gift of emotional cleansing, divinely designed, divinely be-stowed for the here and now. In the there and now, Josh has no need of tears." Morgan concluded,

"Blessed be the God of all comfort; who comforteth us…"

The questions in Leigh's mind overpowered the preacher's voice: *What should I say to Hank? To his mother? To Nancy? Should I say anything to Morgan Kendall and his wife?* She decided to stand by Cassie, behind the family and mourners closer to the grave. She knew Cassie needed her, and the Hodges and Kendalls seemed to be united and strong, as they received condolences, well wishes, and words of appreciation for the eulogy.

Leigh placed her arm around her friend and asked, "Cassie, I told you Hank invited us to eat with the family. Do you feel like eating with them, or would you rather just go home?"

"Really, Leigh, it's your call. I'm fine, just a little emotional, I guess. I really ought to see Hank." Cassie smiled, adding, "Honestly, I am hungry. These days, I'm either wolfing down food or throwing it up."

Leigh answered, "Okay, if you're comfortable enough, we'll just wait here until the crowd has cleared some."

"I believe one of you is Miss Leigh?" Morgan Kendall questioned, as he and his wife approached the waiting girls.

Surprised, Leigh responded, "Oh, Mr. Kendall, I didn't even notice your coming this way. Yes,

Jan Dearman

sir, I'm Leigh Burkhart, and this is our friend Cassie Thompson."

Morgan observed: "Well, I noticed you were very attentive to your friend—you must have been focused, not to have noticed this big old black bear coming your way."

The girls giggled, but their embarrassment was obvious.

"Morgan, stop teasing them." Madeline said, "I'm the old black bear's wife, Madeline. You can call me Maddie. You'll have to excuse my husband—I have been for more than forty years," she laughed.

Cassie smiled in response, and Leigh offered a handshake to Madeline, then to Morgan. "I am pleased to meet you. I know how much Hank admires and appreciates you both. And Mr. Kendall, your words and your voice speaking them were so powerful."

"Yes, Mr. Kendall," Cassie agreed. "It was a beautiful eulogy."

"Why, thank you, Miss Leigh, Miss Cassie. Would you ladies like to walk with us over to the church building? It's time to feed the bears by my account. What do you say?"

Madeline laughed and smacked Morgan's arm, as Cassie said, "Mr. Kendall, right now, I'm feeling mighty bearish myself."

"Well, then, let's growl our way over there." Morgan added, "And I do mean growl. My stomach's making sounds like a whole sleuth of bears!"

Leigh and Cassie waited at the door of the fellowship room, but Mrs. Kendall said, "Morgan and I are going to find seats. We need to rest our old arthritic bones."

"We'll wait here a bit," replied Leigh. "Cassie wants to catch Hank when he comes in. She hasn't had a chance to speak to him."

"Well, good to meet you, missies," Morgan nodded, as he leaned on Madeline's arm and they entered the dining area.

"They are such nice people," Cassie noted. "Do they have to sit by themselves in there?"

"Why, no. Why would they?" Leigh asked.

"Well, lots of times down here the coloreds have to sit apart from the whites. Isn't it that way where you come from?" Cassie asked.

"No! We ride the bus together, go to school together, eat in the same places. That's the way it should be," Leigh defended.

"I agree, Leigh. I'm just saying it's not always that way sometimes in the South."

"Well, Hank says that's the way it should be—we're all just one race, the human race. The color of a man's skin is not important, just what kind of man he is. You've seen what kind of people the Kendalls are—can't find much better than they are."

"You know what, Leigh?" Cassie posed a thought, and Leigh could tell from Cassie's expression she was lit up with a "bright idea."

"What?" Leigh answered, not sure what to expect.

"Well, you know, Morgan Kendall married Hank's parents. Wouldn't it be really neat if he could stay around long enough to marry you and Hank?"

"Cassie, I've still got nearly a year till I graduate," Leigh argued.

"You don't have much more—maybe English and some extra business courses would finish your diploma work. You could even do those before school starts in September," Cassie persisted.

Leigh noticed the Hodges entering the hall to the fellowship area and shushed her friend: "Enough of your air castles, Cassie. Hank and I will do whatever we do when the time's right. Here they come now." Leigh had to admit the suggestion not only was exciting but frightening. Sometimes she did feel abandoned in a juvenile world, while all her closest friends had moved into adulthood, but she wasn't ready for marriage and its responsibilities...*or was she?*

Chapter 45
February 1943

Nancy looked forward to her Friday afternoon visits with Jeff's mother, especially when one of them had received a letter. Mrs. Langston had become a dear friend, and Nancy found her much more independent than Jeff, perhaps, had thought. His mother had found a job selling war bonds. Nancy felt sure she was a valued employee, not only capable, but appreciated for her sweet, friendly disposition.

Nancy and Ethel Langston read Jeff's letters aloud, laughing together at the humor he always managed to find in Army life. While Ethel shared almost all of her letters with Nancy, Nancy refrained from reading the more personal details in hers. Her feelings for Jeff had grown over the months, and Jeff had seemed to be counting on her to be there to welcome him home with open arms.

But, today, once again, Nancy would not be able to share a letter with Mrs. Langston. Nothing had come for her in a few weeks, though Ethel had received two type-written letters, as loving and humorous as ever. Jeffrey said his hands were too weary to hold a pencil and write, but he had access to a typewriter and found it easier to "pound a few lines" on that occasionally. He never could reveal any information about troop movements or his locations; but he guaranteed that, presently, the food was edible, the temperature neither too hot nor too cold, and his bed was as comfortable as the Army had to offer under the circumstances. His letters to his mother had not included any message to give Nancy or any reference to Nancy. It seemed she suddenly was not in his thoughts.

Nancy tried to hide her anxiety about Jeff when Mrs. Langston welcomed her at the door. "Hello, Nancy, please come in. So good to see you as always."

"Thank you, Mrs. Langston," Nancy said, as she entered the room and placed her coat on the hall tree.

"I sense a despondent tone…nothing again this week?" she asked.

"No, ma'am, nothing. How about you?"

"No, nothing more." Mrs. Langston led Nancy back to the kitchen, where she had prepared tea and set cookies on the counter. She continued, "I keep writing to that address we have. I hope he's getting our letters. I'm guessing he may be seeing action somewhere and can't write," Mrs. Langston surmised. "I know he doesn't want me to worry and would write if he could. Good luck with that! I'll be a worrywart till he's safely back home!"

"Yes, ma'am. I know what you mean," Nancy had to admit. She took a seat at the kitchen table, as she stated, "Mrs. Langston, I want you to know I'm going to Atlanta to finish my nurse's training, and I may work there for a while after that. I'll wait and see what happens with the war. I may or may not enlist in the Nurse Corps but finishing up my training and B. S. there will be a plus on my resume if I apply to medical school."

"Oh, Nancy, I'll miss you," Mrs. Langston said, placing the cookies on the table and pouring their cups of tea.

"Yes, ma'am, I'll miss you too. But I'll be coming home from time to time, and I'll certainly see you when I do," Nancy assured her.

Taking a seat across from Nancy, Mrs. Langston asked, "How does your mother feel about this? I'm sure you've been a great help to her in the months since your dad's death."

"Oh, she's agreeable—actually, rather encouraging," Nancy answered. "She knows being in medicine has been my dream since I was a child."

"I know she's so proud of you. Jeff used to say you were the best and brightest in that chemistry class."

Nancy's smile was soft, as she stirred her tea and replied, "Well, that's nice to hear." Changing the subject, Nancy added, "Oh, yes, another factor in my decision, Hank has hinted that he and Leigh may get married after she graduates in May. He's making plans to propose, and mother has done the sweetest thing. She gave Hank my Dad's wedding band to have made into an engagement ring. There'll be enough gold to make a matching wedding band. Hank can't wear one for safety reasons in his work, so I suggested Leigh can put a ring in his nose!"

Mrs. Langston cackled, "Oh, me, the thought!"

"Mother's decided to let them have the house here, and she'll move back to the house on the river. My cousin, Louise, and her husband, Tom, have been living there while building their own place, a 'pay-as-you-go' project. They've done a lot of the work themselves. Now the house is finished, and they're expecting their first child in a few months. Mother wants to be back near the family on the river, in the house where I was born."

"That sounds like a wise decision for your mother. She'll be back where so many of those sweet early marriage memories were made." Mrs. Langston finished her tea. Leaning on the table with her elbows, she rested her chin on her clasped hands. "And so, you have decided to set your sights on the big city and bright lights of Atlanta," Ethel grinned.

Nancy chuckled, "Well, I haven't thought much about big city lights, but more about the advanced training—and the opportunity for medical school right there, if that's what I choose. I'd like to be close enough to home and family to visit regularly, and Atlanta's just an easy train ride away."

Mrs. Langston hesitated, then said, "Nancy, tell me if I am being too nosy, but will you have to work to pay your way through all this training? I'm sure it must be costly."

"No, you're not being too nosy," she laughed, "though I probably wouldn't tell you if you were."

Mrs. Langston shook her head with a chuckle of embarrassment. "Oh, Nancy, you won't do!"

"No, my dad was thoughtful enough to buy some life insurance, just within a couple of years or so before his death. I've wondered if he suspected his heart was failing him. I was with him once, back when I first started college, when he was getting some kind of prescription medicine, likely nitroglycerin tablets like the ones he had with him when he died." Nancy paused, remembering the day at the drugstore soda counter. She sighed, "Well, anyway, Dad made Mother, Hank, and me the joint beneficiaries. It's not a huge amount, but it will get me through until I can start working and pay my own way."

Mrs. Langston said, "Well, please, promise you'll see me before you leave and visit me whenever you can. I am going to miss you."

Nancy answered, "I promise, and I always have looked forward to our Friday afternoons."

"Well, tell me, how is Hank doing with his new job?" Mrs. Langston asked.

"It seems he's doing well. He's getting good training and a decent wage as an apprentice pattern-maker. He seems to have a knack for it. Of course, he's always been excellent at math, mechanical drawing, that sort of thing—really, he's smart and good at most everything. He knows he's contributing to the war effort, because he's been involved in making patterns for tank doors. Since Les is a machinist, Hank feels like he's working with him in a way. Hank's a hard worker, and now that he has the incentive of marrying Leigh, it seems the stage is set for his success."

"Yes," Ethel agreed. "Your mother is likely thinking this is a good time for her to return to her home on the river—you and Hank are now young adults with promising, stable futures."

Nancy took a bite from the peanut butter cookie she had taken from the platter, stating, "I will miss your cookies, too." Her smile betrayed the loss and loneliness she felt, even in the company of Jeff's mother. She wanted to hear from Jeff. She needed to hear from Jeff. But, perhaps, he had gained a new perspective, some objectivity on their relationship, and had determined that, really, it was just a passing flirtation with an available chemistry student. Only time would tell. But time, especially these days, was a capricious commodity, consumed by reckless greed.

Chapter 46

The phone rang, again and again and again. "Would one of you girls, please, answer the phone?!" Rose Burkhart called upstairs. She had walked from the grocer's with bags in both hands and had just managed to open the front door. She had completed her trek to the store in the relative warmth of this winter's day, but her shoes were soaked by the slush of melting snow remaining on the route from the boulevard to their house.

Leigh came bouncing downstairs. "I'll get it, Mom. Sorry. I was storing some things in the attic and didn't hear it till now." She dodged her mother as Rose carried the bags past her to the kitchen. "Whoever it is sure is persistent!" Leigh declared as she picked up the receiver. "Hello?"

Rose returned from the kitchen in stocking feet, having removed her coat and hat, with a cleaning cloth in hand to wipe up wet spots from the hardwood floor. Leigh, excited, flapped her hand in front of Rose to get her attention.

Leigh said, "Oh, my! Really? Yes, thank you, I'll be right there. Yes, it's just wonderful! Thanks for calling." Leigh hung up the phone and grabbed her mother in a big hug. "That was Millie. Cassie just had her baby—a little girl, seven pounds on the nose.

Both mom and baby are healthy, and Cassie's already wanting to see me."

"Oh, Leigh, that's good news! I'm glad we finished the baby girl's dress first. We'll just save the other material for another baby."

"And it's so pretty, Mom. Thanks for your help on it. I'll wrap it up and take it with me to the hospital."

"Okay, dear." Looking at her watch, Rose said, "Better hurry. The downtown bus will be at the stop in twenty minutes."

"I'll just brush my hair and freshen up a bit." Leigh took the stairs two steps at a time, but stopped to add: "Mom, you'll be pleased—the baby's name is Patricia Rose. Isn't that pretty?"

"Why, I'm so pleased Cassie likes my name! Tell her we're so happy for her, and I look forward to holding sweet Patricia Rose in my own hands."

"Will do, Mom." Leigh scaled the stairway and closed the bedroom door behind her.

Rose smiled to herself as she mopped the floor with the cloth and thought about Cassie. *How sad Les can't be with her at such a special, happy time.* She wondered how old Patricia Rose would be before her Daddy could hold her in his arms, before she could attach a living-color person to the black and white face in a photo, to the man described by her mother's words. *What if that can never be?* Rose wondered. She thought many little girls must be growing up only with an ideal man of words and pictures—one whose measure no other man might ever attain. *Oh, how I hate this war!*

Chapter 47

As it had been on those Friday nights, seemingly long ago, the Dynamo Diner was busy and boisterous. There were no post-game cheers and jeers, as during past football seasons. Now, a uniform here and there served as a reminder these were not the same carefree teenagers of 1941; these were young adults growing up in a world that was theirs to save—a world not lost by them, but by adult lust, greed, negligence, hatred—whatever the condemning attitude and motivation man might devise in his heart.

Hank had made peace with himself and the Army's rejection: "Not a character flaw," he had quipped to Leigh, "just a defect in my packaging." She always encouraged him and made him feel like an honorable, responsible man. That took first place on his long list of reasons he loved her. He appreciated Mr. Burkhart's helping him get a job, one Hank found interesting. He was learning and developing skills that, one day, he might use to build his own business, where he could be his own boss and implement changes he thought would be more efficient and productive. Now, he was just on the bottom rung of a long ladder—any input from him likely wouldn't be appreciated.

Hank guided Leigh to the familiar table in the back, where memories lingered warm and bitter-sweet. As requested, Vic had covered the table with a clean white cloth and had placed Hank's bouquet of yellow roses on the table with the place cards arranged at the empty seats: *Les, Cassie, Jeff, Nancy.*

"What is this, Hank?" Leigh asked in bewilderment. "How beautiful!" Leigh touched a place card near her. "But a bit sad, too."

"Well, they would all have been here if they could. But…Happy Valentine's Day, Leigh! It's a couple of days early, but this way even more a surprise." *So far, so great!* Hank thought.

"Oh, Hank, thank you." Leigh kissed his cheek, and they sat at their usual places: Hank and Les at the ends, Leigh and Cassie on one side, and Nancy and Jeff on the other. Only now, four of them were only place cards and wishful thinking. Leigh sighed, "I miss them, don't you?"

"Yes, every day. But I know, wherever they are, they are missing us too. Les is somewhere, wrench in hand, dreaming of eating Dynamo burgers, on the house, with little Patty Rose; Nancy is in Atlanta, seeing humans in hospital gowns, at their most vulnerable and unattractive; Cassie is at home, changing diapers and wiping spit up off her shoulder; and Jeff…well, he's probably somewhere wearing goggles, hiding his Egghead under a helmet."

Leigh chuckled. "I guess that pretty well sums it up." She took Hank's hand and, again, said, "Thanks, Hank. This was such a thoughtful early Valentine's Day."

He answered, "You are very welcome. But the night is young," he declared.

Vic brought their usual sodas to the table in elegant goblets. Noticing Leigh's questioning look, he said, "This table looks too nice for ordinary soda glasses." Leigh laughed, as he asked, "Can I interest you in something special, or is it the usual?"

Hank replied, "What could be more special than the usual? Okay with you, Leigh?"

"My sentiment exactly, Vic," she agreed.

"Two Dynamo burgers with all the trimmings and fries coming up," Vic stated and went to the kitchen.

"Have you heard from Nancy?" Leigh asked.

"She called briefly to let us know she was settling into her apartment. I think she's eager to begin her studies and training. Maybe it will take her mind off Jeff. She hasn't heard from him in quite a while. She's beginning to think she had read too much into their relationship, though his letters did have some pretty romantic stuff going on."

"You read them?" Leigh asked, surprised.

"Oh, no," he defended, "she read some bits to me—wanted my opinion—did I think he was sincere, honest, whatever."

"Did you?" she pursued.

"Well, like I told her, a guy who said some of the things he put in writing would have to be some kind of heel not to mean them, especially if he knows how she feels."

Leigh sighed, "Maybe she'll hear from him soon, or find there is a reasonable explanation. Cassie receives letters fairly regularly, and Les is near the front. Mail seems to get where it's intended—if it's sent."

Hank confided to Leigh, "I hope for Nancy's sake, she can just get into her work and be distracted for a while. She's close to Mrs. Langston. She will be the first to get information, and she will be in contact with Nancy. Mrs. Langston promised, even if the news is not good, even if Jeff is missing or has lost interest, she will tell Nancy." With a wry smile, Hank continued, "If Jeff has lost interest, the friendship between Mrs. Langston and Nancy will be pretty uncomfortable."

"I should imagine so," Leigh affirmed.

"My friends, here are your entrees!" Vic announced. Playing the proper waiter, dishtowel over his arm, he placed a china platter of burgers and fries in front of them, with matching individual dinner plates. "No celebration like this can be served on our common restaurant ware."

"Oh, Vic, you and Hank have made every-thing so nice," Leigh responded. "Thank you."

"My pleasure," Vic announced, "but the night is young," he declared, throwing the dishtowel over his shoulder.

Hank and Leigh laughed at his histrionics, and she asked Hank, "Where have I heard that be-fore?"

They enjoyed their meal in the security of love and the ease of friendship. It was almost like it had been in the days before—before the world was turned upside down, before young lives fast-for-warded into brief adulthoods, before friends were just names and memories on artfully trimmed card stock.

Their meals finished, Hank sat back in his chair and asked, "Well, bring me up to date on what's going on at good old North Side High."

On cue, the juke box interrupted and began playing Harry James' number one hit, "I Had the Craziest Dream."

"Oh, listen, Hank. I just love that song. It's so romantic," Leigh gushed.

The words hardly had passed Leigh's lips, when Vic arrived with another platter, this one cov-ered. "Dessert this evening is on the house—a new special, chocolate pudding cake with a scoop of ice cream—one dessert, two spoons," he declared.

"Thanks, Vic, you're a gem!" Hank declared, with a sly laugh, as Vic set the platter in front of them and removed the cover. Next to the dessert was a small velvet box. Hank picked it up, scooted his chair away from the table, and dropped to one knee before Leigh, who gasped and put her hands over her mouth. People in the nearby tables took notice, and chain whispers spread through the restaurant, silencing voices. Only Harry James continued his serenade in the background.

"Leigh Burkhart, I have told you I love you and want you to be my partner in life. Now, in this most romantic of all places..." He grinned as unrestrained giggles popped up here and there. "...I ask you to be my wife." Hank opened the box to reveal a simple gold band centered by an emerald cut topaz, Leigh's birthstone.

Leigh waited so long to speak Hank wondered if he had been a presumptuous fool.

"Yes," Leigh whispered through her hands. Then, she wrapped her arms around Hank's neck and declared, "Yes, yes, I will be your wife." The diner erupted in applause, cheers, and whistles. Hank and Leigh stood, their arms wrapped around each other. Leigh leaned against Hank's chest and, before their audience, Hank raised a clenched fist in victory, de-claring, "She said 'Yes'!"

For those at this time, in this place, the world could be, for a moment, right and good and full of hope.

Chapter 48

Nancy adjusted her apron and cap and proceeded at a fast clip to the nurses' station, where she was to report to observe rounds. She prayed her first day of real patient interaction and assessment went as well as her class work—that the practice would be as successful as the theory, that her foundation of knowledge would be practical and not just book-learning.

"Miss Hodge?" asked the Senior Nurse, as Nancy approached the counter.

"Yes, ma'am, Nurse Phillips," Nancy read from her name badge. "I was told to report to you for further instruction."

"Good. You're punctual. Nurse Danley will be here shortly. You are assigned to accompany her on her rounds. You may have minimal interaction with each patient—just friendly conversation, but no involvement with treatment or care. That's only for the licensed nurse. You will take notes and give a daily report on what you have observed—what was done for the patient, why it was done, and any observations or comments you think appropriate. You will submit your report the next morning that you are assigned observation. Understand?"

"Yes, ma'am." Nancy replied, filing all instructions away in the securest part of her mind.

"Here is a clipboard with forms you may use for your notes. They have helpful guidelines on important things to observe. Have a pen?" she asked.

"Yes, ma'am," Nancy patted the leather purse hanging from her shoulder.

"Good. Prepared." Noticing an approaching nurse, Nurse Phillips said, "Miss Hodge, this is Nurse Danley." Nancy turned to greet an attractive petite woman, with dark hair, even darker brown eyes, and a welcoming smile. Nancy thought, *Good ... finally a nurse with a friendly face.*

"Good morning, Miss Hodge," Nurse Danley chirped. "Welcome to the floor."

"Why, thank you," Leigh replied. I'm so pleased to begin this part of my training."

"Well, today, we're nearing full capacity. You'll see we nurses often have to put the pedal to the metal, as they say, but be careful never to run off the road."

"Yes, ma'am, I'm sure that's how it can be," Nancy smiled.

"Okay, let's move," she said, pulling a stethoscope from her pocket and draping it around her neck. As she led Nancy down the hall, Nurse Danley said under her voice, "You don't have to call me 'ma'am' or 'Nurse Danley,' unless we are around Nurse Phillips. She's a stickler from way back. I'm Sara."

Nancy chuckled, "Okay, Sara, got it."

It was nearly one o'clock, Nancy's feet were aching, and her note sheets were filling fast, when Sara said, "I think we can rest for a while in the nurses' break room. Did you bring something for lunch?"

"Sure did," she answered, patting her purse again. But I don't have a drink."

"No problem," Sara waved her hand. We keep coffee going all the time and juice and sodas in the fridge."

With time limited, Nancy wasted no time in finishing her sandwich and juice, but Sara had already cleaned her place at the small pedestal table and was saying, "Tell me about yourself, Nancy."

Nancy gave a brief description of her family, their home, and how her father had made her Atlanta training possible after his death.

"They sound like wonderful people," Sara said. "No husband, no boyfriend?"

"No, afraid not," Nancy answered. "Got close once, I thought, but it seems it hasn't worked out." Nancy wondered why she said that to this stranger, but Sara seemed so open and caring, it was just drawn out of her. *Probably a good trait for a nurse*, Nancy thought.

Sara stood and said, "Got to get back at it." As they walked from the break room, she confided, "Between you and me, Nancy, we nurses are lucky to find time for a break to eat or go to the bathroom. She laughed, "Some of us have been known to do both at the same time in under five minutes!"

Nancy restrained her laughter as they passed the nurses station and Sara nodded to the grim visage of Nurse Phillips and said quietly through her teeth, "Hello, Nurse Phillips, please, forgive us for smiling." Nancy already liked this funny, joyful little person. Nancy noted that, while Sara brought cheer to every room she entered, she also brought the best, most efficient, professional skills. Nancy thought Sara would be an excellent model not only of care, but of caring.

As they neared the end of their rounds, Sara said, "We have a couple of surgical patients who were transferred from the Army hospital. We had the specialists to address their specific problems, one an open thoracic wound and the other a shrapnel injury to the eyes. They stopped at the first room and Sara pulled the chart from the rack at the door. Corporal Dandridge, 23 years old, had treatment for an open chest wound at a field hospital in New Guinea. When stabilized sufficiently for med flight, he was brought Stateside to the Army hospital here in Atlanta, and almost immediately transferred to us for surgery to stem infection threatening his lungs and heart." Sara said aside, "Besides, the wards over there are like cans of sardines."

Nancy waited at a distance, while Sara proceeded to the hospital bed with a cheery, "Well, Corporal Dandridge, how are you doing today?" He opened his eyes and gave a thumbs-up, while Sara took his blood pressure and listened to his heart through the pads and gauze surrounding his chest. She checked his IV and said, "I'll be back in a few minutes to change that out for you. Are you comfortable enough?"

The soldier whispered, "Okay."

Sara advised, "Well, if you feel the pain is more than you can handle, you just press the buzzer under your finger. I have orders to up your dosage if necessary. Okay?"

With a weak smile, Dandridge gave another thumbs-up.

In the hall outside, Sara charted the visit with the patient before returning the clipboard to the rack.

Nancy asked, "What's his prognosis?"

She answered in a lowered voice, "I can't say for sure. Judging from experience and observations, maybe three days."

Nancy began to ask, "Three days...?"

Sara interrupted her, "They did all they could. Three days." Nancy must have looked troubled, for

Sara added, "That's war. There are Dandridges all over the globe. Our job is to give ours the best care and comfort we can—and hold ourselves together so we can keep on doing it as long as they keep coming. Think you can handle that?"

"Yes, it's just so sad," Nancy responded.

Sara looked at Nancy for a moment, then said, "Yeah." She paused, then said, "Let's check the next one. She pulled the chart from the rack. Another Corporal, this one Langston…"

Nancy interrupted, "Langston?"

"Yep," said Sara, "Corporal Langston, Jeffrey…"

Nancy, feeling faint, backed against the wall for support.

"What's wrong? You know him?" asked Sara.

Nancy could only nod, then whispered, "He's the one—the one that didn't work out…or I thought it didn't. He stopped writing."

Sara said, "Nancy, you may want to skip this visit. It's too personal, too emotional."

"No," Nancy said, taking a deep breath. "I can do this. I'm supposed to be quiet and out of the way."

"Well, okay," Sara agreed. "But if you think you're going to lose control, you just get out of there fast."

Nancy nodded. "Sara, can you explain what's wrong? Will he live?"

Sara began, "I probably shouldn't give you this information considering the circumstances, but his condition is not life threatening—perhaps, quality of life threatening. He hasn't been able to write you because he hasn't been able to see. Langston has a shrapnel injury that required very delicate ophthalmologic surgery. He has lost almost all vision in one eye. With the surgery, time and healing, vision in the other eye may return. We'll know when the bandages come off in a week or two."

"At least he'll live," sighed Nancy.

"Yes, he'll go on breathing, and his heart will keep beating, but he's depressed. That's my main concern about this patient. Sometimes patients like him believe they'd be better off dead. Part of our job is to help them think about possibilities, not limitations."

"Let me be there. I can handle this. Maybe somehow I can help."

"Okay, here we go," said Sara. "Hold it together."

Nancy nodded and followed Sara into the room. Jeff's long, thin form lay motionless under the bedsheet, his eyes swathed in bandages. Nancy noticed his curly dark hair had been buzzed to Army standards but was beginning to grow out. The radio on the table next to him was playing soft big band music. Nancy remained close to the door and watched as Sara went about her tasks with her cheery words: "Corporal Langston, how are you feeling today? I notice you didn't eat your lunch. You need to get some meat back on those bones. You'll be getting those bandages off before long, and we don't want you to look puny when we discharge you."

Sara was straightening and tucking the sheets at the foot of the bed when Jeff ordered, "Leave it."

"Corporal Langston, I'm just doing my job," she declared. "I'll leave when I'm finished."

"Who made you commanding officer?" he asked derisively.

"Self-appointed—the best woman for the job," she retorted.

It seemed Jeff sensed another presence in the room and asked, "Is somebody with you?"

"Just my second in command, a student nurse observing how to deal with a difficult patient. She's just supposed to take notes and stay quiet." Sara turned and winked at Nancy.

"Well, hurry up, get out, and leave me alone," Jeff barked.

"Langston, are you this sweet and gentlemanly to all your women back home?"

"There aren't any women back home," he muttered.

"Now, Langston, everybody's got a mother. And a good looking fellow like you must have a girl waiting for him to get out of here and come home to her."

"No. Nobody." He turned his face away from her voice and muttered again, "Get out."

"Well, our shift is about over. We hate to leave your sparkling company. I'll be back tomorrow, and we'll chat some more."

There was no response as Sara and Nancy left the room. They had moved down the hall a few paces, when Sara said, "I'll clock out. Then let's go to the break room and talk."

Nancy was waiting with a cup of coffee in hand when Sara joined her and said, "Good job in there of holding it together. I know that wasn't easy."

Nancy searched for words and replied, "Sara, you just don't know how great it was to see him alive. His mother had received only a couple of typed letters a few weeks back and then nothing, and I hadn't heard anything since before that. We assumed he was unable to write, in conflict somewhere." Nancy smiled. "I guess he is—he's here, unable to write, and in conflict with himself."

"Astute observation," said Sara.

Pensive, Nancy then smiled, remembering Jeff's message to his mother. "You may find this amusing: Jeff told his mother he was where the food

291

was edible, the temperature wasn't too hot or cold, and his bed was as comfortable as the Army had, given the circumstances." Sara grinned, and Nancy said, "That's Jeff's sense of humor. He must have been at the field hospital when someone typed those letters for him. I guess his humor and hope are running low right now."

Sara offered some encouragement: "Nancy, Jeff has been without sight ever since he was wounded, and that's been a long time now. He knows the surgery gave promise of improvement. But even now, no one knows for sure—not even the best ophthalmologist in Atlanta. When those bandages come off, if his vision—at least, enough functional vision, has been restored, we may see a quick improvement in his attitude."

Nancy replied, "Thanks, Sara. You know, in this first day I've known you, a day that's turned out to be so important to me, you've become pretty special."

Sara looked down at her folded hands on the pedestal table. "Well, it's sweet of you to say that. Guess I'm an incurable romantic," she declared with a smile. "Since I am now privy to—and aiding and abetting the keeping of your secret identity from Jeff, I'll tell you something about myself, about my motivation for loving my job and feeling it's the most important thing this little old Atlanta gal can do." She collected her thoughts and tried to find the right words. "I try to give all my patients the care they need, but the military guys who sometimes are transferred over here—like Jeff and Dandridge—well, they are extra special. You see, I came back home to Atlanta after Pearl Harbor. I was a civilian nurse. My husband was a corpsman on the Arizona."

Nancy understood the implication of her words and said, "Sara, I'm so sorry. How do you find the strength, the courage? Every man like Jeff or Dandridge must be a painful reminder."

"No, Nancy…well, perhaps, in a way…especially a sweet guy like Dandridge," she admitted. "But every guy like them motivates me to do my best, give my best, even if that means slapping one like Jeff up the side of the head—not really, of course—but, to make him see he still has time and life to use as best he can. Right now, Jeff's depressed and withdrawn because he thinks he won't be able to return to his old life and do the things he used to do. He's even shut you out, believing you wouldn't want a defective Jeff."

"But that's not true. And he wouldn't be 'defective'—just vision-impaired, and we could deal with that."

Sara stated, "Try telling that to a man like him."

"And I may, when you tell me the time is right to make my presence known."

Sara nodded. "We'll see how it goes." She stood to leave. "I need to get home. Tomorrow's shift comes early, and I have a cat that loves me like a dog," she smiled. Sara leaned over Nancy with both hands on the table and added, "Nancy, I know my Bill clung to that last breath with all the will he had, because our life together was so precious to him. Jeff needs to realize, if you love him, your life together can be precious. He needs to see that, even if he can see nothing else … if you get my drift," she concluded with a grin. "See you Wednesday."

Nancy walked to her apartment in the chill of the early evening. She knew Mrs. Langston should know about Jeff, if she could only make his mother understand the importance of giving him time to heal from the surgery and from his depression. She decided she would take the train to Chattanooga Friday, if she could get a ticket, and return after worship with the family on Sunday. If she could see Mrs. Langston on Saturday, talk to her face-to face, tell her exactly what had happened, she might be able to prevent her rushing down to Atlanta to see her son, which likely would have a negative impact on Jeff—and Nancy's relationship with him, and surely, would disappoint his mother.

Well, what did I learn today? Nancy asked herself. *So much—almost too much to process.* Of course, the customary nursing procedures and tasks she already knew were confirmed by observing the capable, efficient Nurse Danley. *Such a dear...a great nurse...and strong! I don't know...Could I be like that? To think of Jeff's life ending in such a hor-rific way...I would have nightmares the rest of my life.* Then Nancy realized: *She may...There may be hundreds, thousands of wives jarred out of restful sleep by the sights and sounds of war playing in their heads. How I hate this war!*

Chapter 49

Nancy held Ethel's hand. The doctor's voice was soft, but commanding: "Mrs. Langston, we are going to remove your son's bandages in a few minutes. We won't know if surgery has been successful, until we assess Jeff's reaction. If some vision has been restored, initially, there should be awareness of light. Perhaps, he will see shapes, blurred images, colors that, we hope, will clarify given an indefinite time— days, weeks. We have explained all of this to Jeff. If the surgery has failed, if sufficient vision has not been restored, his depression may deepen. We will recommend counseling and therapy specific to vision loss. Awareness of your presence in that event might be detrimental to him psychologically. You and Nancy may be present in the room, but silent. I trust we will have a good indication of a positive outcome within the first five minutes or so. Can you do that for me…for Jeff?"

"Yes, doctor. Nancy has been preparing me for this," she responded.

"Thank you, Mrs. Langston." The doctor looked at Nancy and nodded his approval, with the words, "Good job, Nurse Hodge."

Nancy and Ethel continued to hold hands and lingered inside the door as they watched the doctor's careful snipping and removal of the bandage. Layer by interminable layer, the gauze encircling Jeff's head was removed with care and precision, until remaining were only the heavy gauze pads covering his eyes.

"Nurse Danley, lower the lights, please." Sara turned off the lights and tilted the blinds to lessen the sunlight coming into the room. "Thank you." The doctor addressed Jeff: "Now, Jeff I am going to remove the pads, as I told you. Don't be concerned if your vision is not normal, as you remembered. If you sense light, that's a good sign. After a few minutes, if you see movement, then blurred forms, perhaps, colors, that will be an even better sign. Understand?"

Jeff whispered, "Yes."

Nancy could only imagine Jeff's fear and his mother's anxiety. Nancy was prayerful, hopeful, but her days of silent nearness to Jeff had only confirmed that, regardless of his sight, her life was with him. Whether she walked with him in the light or guided him through the darkness, she wanted to be by his side.

"Jeff, keep your eyes closed until I have removed both pads and give further directions," the doctor ordered. He gently loosened the tape around one pad until he could lift it from Jeff's face, then repeated the procedure on the other side. "Nurse, make a note. The exterior lacerations have healed nicely, clean and free of any sign of infection. Now, Jeff, open your eyes."

Jeff opened his eyes slowly and blinked. "Nothing…there's nothing," he moaned.

"Wait, Jeff, be patient. Nurse Danley, open the blinds some more."

"Yes, doctor," she replied, glancing at Ethel, whose hand covered her mouth, and Nancy, now with her arm around Jeff's mother.

Jeff blinked again. "There's light … I see light!"

The doctor smiled. "Good, Jeff, that's good."

They all waited, not speaking, for what seemed more like hours than seconds. The doctor waved his hand in front of Jeff's eyes, and Jeff waved, "Back at you—is that you, Doc?"

The doctor hung his head in relief and laughed, "Yes, Jeff, it's Doc." Again, they waited. Then, the doctor said, "Nurse Danley, let's give Jeff some more light. Just flip the switch," he chuckled. "Jeff, what now?"

"What now, Doc?" Jeff grinned. "That's a memorable question." Nancy had to step out into the hall, missing Jeff's response: "Doc, everything's blurry,

298

but I think I see your white coat…and there's more white over there…the nurse?"

The doctor sighed. "Jeff, this is a positive indication that you are regaining vision—perhaps not completely back to normal, but certainly improved. We'll give you a few weeks of recuperation, then do some tests, and we can give you a better prognosis. You must be patient. It may take some time to maximize your vision. And, of course, glasses, perhaps other devices, may help you function almost normally."

"Thanks, Doc." Jeff felt for the doctor's hand and gave it a firm shake. "You've given me something to *look* forward to…no pun intended."

The doctor grinned and motioned for Jeff's mother to approach the bed. "Jeff, there is someone here you may want to *see*…pun intended," he retorted.

Ethel went to her son, held his hand, and said, "Jeffrey, how I've missed you."

"Mom…you're here." Jeff sniffed and said, "Mom, I want to cry, but I'm afraid I'll do damage."

The doctor interrupted, "Tears may sting a bit, Jeff, but they can't hurt you."

"No need to cry, son. This is a good day. I hope we can get you home soon and you can rest and recuperate there."

Again, the doctor interrupted. "Mrs. Langston, as soon as all his paperwork is completed, we can release Jeff to go home. There are some good doctors in Chattanooga who can follow up with his treatment, even some rehab and occupational therapy. I can have his files sent there."

"That would be wonderful," Ethel replied. "Just so wonderful."

Jeff grasped her hand and put it to his lips. "Love you, Mom."

"I love you too, Jeff."

Nancy was pacing in the hall when she heard Sara call her name. Nancy stopped but didn't reply.

Sara came to her and said, "Nancy, come back in. It'll be okay now. Jeff has hope, he's going home before long, and now all he needs is you."

"Sara, I'm afraid I'll upset him. I have basically lied to him all this time, skulking around his room. He'll know I've seen him at his worst…It may be too upsetting…too…unforgiveable."

"Nancy, if he's the man you said he was, the man you think he still is, if he knows you have stuck by him, even seen him at his worst…and you still want him, surely, that has to be a good thing." She took Nancy's hand, "Come on, girl, trust Nurse Danley. You're going to do this."

Sara spoke to the doctor for permission and then went to Jeff's bedside. "Jeff, this is your friend, Nurse Danley—the one who's enjoyed our daily tete-a-tete chats."

"Nurse Danley, you're a lot of bossiness in a small package, from what I can tell," Jeff teased.

"Well, he does have a sense of humor after all," Sara declared. "Well, you've been pretty sullen and cranky—not the worst I've had, but in the top ten, I'd say."

"Guess I own you an apology," Jeff admitted.

"No, not really, I'd probably been out of sorts, too, to have gone through everything you have. But now, it's time to get a grip and move on. What do you say?"

"I say, you're in charge, like always," he laughed.

"You got that right, buster. Now, remember, my second-in-command? She's about the best nurse trainee I've ever had. She's been here, lo, these many days—silent, just taking notes, observing, learning how to deal with cranky corporals—but, most of all, praying for you. I think you ought to thank her personally."

Sara looked at Nancy and mouthed, "Come here." Sara moved away as Nancy took her place at the bed.

"You are the nurse to whom I must apologize, it seems," Jeff said. He frowned and tilted his head, as if to see her better. "Are you going to introduce yourself."

"No, but I'll give you a clue, a memorable question…What now, Corporal Langston?"

Jeff's cheeks glistened with tears, as he reached out to her. "Nancy?…Nancy…It's been you all this time?"

"Yes, Jeff. I've been here. You've had some bad, cranky days, but I've loved you even then." Nancy leaned close to him and asked, "What now?" She kissed him and said, "That was the second in a long time, but only the first of many more in the time to come."

Chapter 50
January 1944

Leigh sat on the living room floor and played with Patty Rose, who had taken her first baby steps just the previous week. The child was bright, beautiful, and strong. She looked so much like Cassie but had Les' blonde hair and blue eyes. Leigh loved this little girl so much she couldn't imagine someday loving her own child even more.

Cassie, sitting on the sofa, continued reading the recent letter from Les: "…Thanks for the new picture of you and Patty Rose—the two most beautiful women in the world, and they're all mine. (All you GIs out there, eat your hearts out!)" Cassie, shaking her head, looked at Leigh and grinned. "As usual, I can't say where we are, except we've come from a place of warmth and beauty to the misery of almost daily clouds, rain, and muck. Of course, memories of my sweet Cassie outshine the first, and even now, you are my rainbow." She folded the letter and returned it to her pocket. "There's more, but that's just for me."

Leigh caught Patty Rose before she could fall against the coffee table. "Wow, who would have thought Les had this poetic side to him?"

Cassie replied, "This war must have brought it out. It seems each letter is a little shorter, but more…well… poetic, like you said." Cassie giggled. "You know, when he comes back, we may be a disappointment, when we don't fit the image in his head. I'm still carrying some extra pounds after the baby, and Patty Rose is not all sweetness and light—she poops and pukes and stretches my last nerve sometimes with her crying." Cassie laughed. "Remember Hank, the 'nerve-frayer'?"

Leigh chuckled, "Oh, yes, he left here about seven o'clock this morning!"

Patty Rose had plopped down on her stomach and was rubbing her eyes. Leigh gathered the baby in her arms and sat cross-legged, cuddling her, countering, "Oh, she is sweetness and light. She can just come stay with Auntie Leigh anytime and let Mommy unwind in a long, hot bubble bath."

"Mind if I get that in writing?" Cassie asked.

"Sure, let me get a pen," Leigh declared. Laying her head on Leigh's shoulder, the baby snuggled against her and seemed to settle down to rest. "I think she's played out," Leigh whispered.

"Do you want to lay her down on the blanket over here," Cassie asked, patting the space next to her on the couch.

"Not as long as she's content right here," Leigh answered. Leigh stroked Patty Rose's hair and rubbed her back, while Cassie observed the pair with a loving and wistful smile.

Cassie resumed their conversation, asking, "When do you start your new job?"

"Bright and early Monday morning. I'm eager to get started. Hank's working almost every day, even part of Saturdays. The only variation in a day for me is what I fix for dinner."

"I'll know more about that when Les gets back and we have our own place. You know, I'm glad I decided to stay with his parents. Your talk of sharing an apartment was exciting, but Mrs. Thompson has been a real help. She and Mr. Thompson let us have our privacy, but we're invited to join them for dinner every evening—that's really nice. We usually stay upstairs till Patty's bedtime." She paused before adding, "I know Les would be pleased to see how much they enjoy their granddaughter."

Leigh commented: "Hank will be a good father someday. Right now, he's tied up with his job, and I'll work till I get pregnant."

"What will you be doing at the TNT plant?" Cassie inquired.

Leigh answered, "Well, it sounds like a cushy job—'executive secretary' in the office for one of the big guys. I'm thankful for all those business courses that finished my requirements—and for good English skills. Of course, if I have to do more than add 'two plus two,' I may be in hot water."

Cassie agreed, "Yeah, you weren't the brightest light in geometry, but at times I wondered if it just might be a ploy to get Hank to help you."

"No," Leigh grinned, "that was just the one benefit of taking the class." Leigh continued, "Patty Rose is really growing. She's gaining weight I can tell."

"Want me to take her?" asked Cassie.

"No, but you may have to help me get up off the floor, when she wakes up." Leigh chuckled but lowered her voice when the baby sighed and rubbed her nose. "Shh, sweet baby," she whispered. "Did I tell you the plant will provide chauffeur service if I have to work late?"

"No, you didn't," Cassie replied. "Ooh, aren't you special!" she teased.

"Well, not just for me, in particular, but for any of the office staff. Of course, I'll take the bus most of the time."

The friends sat in comfortable silence, and Cassie became pensive. "I was thinking the other day, we're all in this war in some way—not like Les is, I know, but playing a part—you and Hank in businesses directly supporting the Allies, Nancy in nursing…Of course, Jeff is still in the war in a way. And every day when I wake up, I think about Les, where he is, what he may be doing—and I pray. I look at Patty Rose, and I know my part in the war is to bring this child up to be grateful for what she has…for her Daddy and men like him, who love their babies but have to leave them…to make a bad world better." Cassie's voice quivered. "Patty Rose's part is to give hope…just give some hope…that everything can be better, when Daddy comes home."

Leigh hugged the baby and waited, praying, while Cassie wept.

Chapter 51
November 1944

*D*ear *Hank (a.k.a. Junior Buddy),*

You haven't heard from me in months—sorry about that, but our workdays have been kind of busy and long—and noisy! If I could only tell you all the places I've been, you'd be impressed. But seeing the world like this, you miss most of the tourist sites—or they're disappointing. And you don't get pretty travel stickers for your luggage! I can tell you I have no desire to visit Omaha, Nebraska. It's probably miserable and flat and a good place to grow corn, but not much else. (No offense to my Nebraskan comrades).

I am writing to tell you I'm in an Army Hospital in Paris, recuperating from a skirmish with the opposing team. Now don't get worried. I still have all my major limbs and vital parts, and obviously, my clever wit is intact. But CG Patton is kicking me out, honorably, and maybe even with a few doodads Patty Rose can pin on her favorite doll. They're sending me back to Benning to finish up paperwork, and then I'll catch a slow bus or a fast train home—maybe the Chattanooga Choo Choo can choo choo me home.

I'm not sure when that will be, hopefully, by Thanksgiving.

Hank, I haven't told Cass. There is no point in her being worried. I'll be gimpy and thin, but still as good-looking as ever (he said with a winning smile!). Please don't say anything to her or the folks. I sure would appreciate your picking me up and bringing Cass and the baby when you come to the station. I look forward to seeing everyone but waiting to see Cassie and Patty is nearly driving me nuts! I want to have a little time with them, even before seeing Mom and Dad.

As soon as I'm in the States and know my plans, I'll call you. Thanks, Hank. You know I love you, Junior Bud!

Always, Les

Chapter 52
Tuesday, November 21, 1944

"Leigh, you've made some nice changes around the house," Eliza remarked, as she placed dishes on the dining room table. "You have a knack for decorating."

Setting the last piece of silverware by the dinner plates, Leigh said, "Thanks, Mrs. Hodge." She grinned, "You're a tough act to follow. Really the credit goes to *Decorating for You*, by Florence Terhune. She says one should welcome her guests into a home with 'singing tones of a colorful setting.'"

Eliza laughed. "Well, you've learned her lessons well, I would say. And aren't you the brave one, having what, twelve, for dinner and cooking all this delicious food by yourself? The smells from the kitchen are amazing."

"Not quite that many," Leigh answered. "Mom and Dad are visiting family in Chicago, and Millie and Alice had other plans. But, with Hank and Jeff, it's still cooking for twelve!"

Hank opened the door to Cassie's knock, with "Come on in. Now, we can get this party started!" Cassie greeted Nancy and Jeff, who were sitting together on the couch, dropped her diaper bag and jacket on the nearest chair, and delivered Patty Rose into Nancy's outstretched arms. She entered the dining room to offer her assistance: "Anything I can do?" Looking at the table and the crystal bowl centerpiece of fresh, colorful, seasonal mums, she continued, "That you haven't done already? Wow, you've been a busy Leigh bee!"

"Yes, but I've had fun. I asked off this week to get ready for three days of cooking and feasting—well, four, if you count Leftovers Friday. Saturday I'll start my diet." Leigh returned to the kitchen, calling behind her, "Cassie, you want some hot apple cider or coffee, or something for Patty Rose? It will be about half an hour till the food's ready?"

Cassie followed Leigh and said, "I'll take some cider, but Patty Rose is fine. She had a bottle on our way over." Anticipating a remark from Leigh, Cassie said, "And, I know, I know, it's time to start weaning her off the bottle, but she enjoys it so much. It's calming—why rock the boat?" she laughed.

Hank and Jeff were setting up the card table and chairs for extra seating in front of the living room window when the phone rang. Hank raced to take the call, as he had so many times in recent days, but this time, he heard the welcome greeting, "Hey, Junior Buddy."

Hank said, "You don't know how great it is to hear those condescending words! Where are you?"

"I'm sitting on a bench in Terminal Station, about as antsy as a man can get. How soon can you be here?"

"We'll leave as soon as I can gather up your girls. Hang tight!"

"Drive safely," Les warned, and the connection clicked off.

Hank picked up Patty Rose and her doll from the floor in front of Nancy and called Cassie from the kitchen. "Cass, we've got time before we eat, and I have a surprise for Patty Rose. Come go with us. She may get upset without her mom."

"A surprise? What kind of surprise? You better not be spending more money on her. Leigh's told me some of the things you've put in Santa's bag. You're going to spoil her."

"Just come on. Quit yapping!" he commanded.

Thankfully, the traffic was light, and they arrived at the terminal in less than twenty minutes. As they pulled up in front of the station and parked on the street, Cassie said, "Oh, I know, they're lighting the big tree tonight. Patty Rose will be excited." She scooped up the baby, got out of the sedan, and started up the walkway to enter the massive arched entrance. Hank followed close behind.

Jan Dearman

Hank saw Les first, one among several uni-
formed men milling about the terminal. Hank saw his
friend was thin, pale and listed to one side, supported
by a cane. Cassie was looking around for a Christmas
tree, when her gaze fell upon her husband, and she
waited so long to move, Hank wondered, *Does she
even recognize him?* Hank's restraint melted when
Cassie raced to embrace Les. He smiled through his
tears. *They're just one big hug!*

Chapter 53

Nancy looked at her friends and family gathered around the table and remembered the words of her father: "I am sad and fearful when I think of the challenges and dangers that may lie ahead…I pray God will shield you from harm—or heal you from injury if that should happen. And I pray, when this awful war is behind us, we all may still be here, together at this table, as a family, to thank God for allowing it to be so."

Now, they were all there, with the addition of Jeff and a little girl, who was love and joy and hope. The only one missing was the man whose love for Eliza McNeal had made this scene possible. But Josh's prayer was answered: Hank, now at the head of the table, had been shielded from harm. Les had survived, and Jeff was healing from injury. And though the awful war had not ended, it seemed to be waning and losing its thirst for the blood of young men and women, their youth stolen and replaced by cares, responsibilities, and wisdom beyond their years. Then, Nancy's gaze fell upon her mother, and she reminded herself: *Mother is strength and courage*. She smiled. *Mother is a McNeal woman.*

CPSIA information can be obtained
at www.ICGtesting.com
Printed in the USA
LVHW032246100322
712904LV00006B/333

9 781949 472479